He Wasn't Good Enough for Me

By: Jenay Balderas

HE WASN'T GOOD ENOUGH FOR ME

HE WASN'T GOOD ENOUGH FOR ME

Table of Contents

HE WASN'T GOOD ENOUGH FOR ME

Acknowledgments:

First, I would like to thank my husband, Jose, for his encouragement and support.
I want to thank my mother Monique, my sister, Destine and my two coworkers and friends Eliza and Karen for reading over chapters, throwing ideas at me and being a part of this new venture in my life. Also, I want to thank my really good friend Lizet for her support. Thank you all.

Jazelle Henry

Preface

I used to be a good and honest woman. I used to be so completely devoted to my husband. Our lives used to be so peaceful. But now, things are different. Now my life has been flipped upside down and I have no idea if I can even fix it. Everything that I once loved and adored in my life is now fighting against me. I don't even know if this is a battle that I can win. When I met my husband, we were both 18 years old. He was everything that I thought a man should be. He was so damn fine, and he was so good and loyal to me. He was down for me and whatever I wanted I got. But now I'm 28, and all that I have ever known was Antonio. And quite frankly I've become bored with the married life. Lately I've felt like not only am I the center of his world, but I am his entire world. And even though that may sound nice, it's not. It's suffocating. I just can't get with that.

I want a new high. A new thrill. A new man. Even though, in the beginning I tried to fight it, I felt like I had found just what I was looking for. I know y'all think I'm wrong and that I should have stayed faithful to my husband but honestly, I couldn't care less what anyone thinks. It's been time for me to be my own person. I needed to experience life outside of Antonio. Don't get me wrong. I do still love my husband. But I felt like if I did not do this, I would have resented him for the rest of our boring ass lives. I needed to do this for me.

Now, at this very moment, I know that everything is not what it seems. I know now that not everyone is who they portray themselves to be. Not even the people that you feel you know the best. I don't know exactly at what point my life went to shit. But I'll let y'all figure all of that out. So take a ride with me. Witness my life and the lives of those around me in this tale of betrayal that ruined me.

Jazelle Henry

Riiing Riiinnnng Riiiiinnng

The ringing of my phone shook me out of my daydream. I looked at the phone and saw it was Karli. I knew she didn't want anything but to try to get me out of the house. It was Friday night, my kids were gone with my mama, and Antonio, my husband, was asleep.

"Hello." I answered the phone

"Biiiitch lets go to the Highlands tonight," Karli screamed into the phone.

"Go to the highlands for what? There ain't nothing to do over there, but eat and watch a movie, that's a date bitch. I do not want to date you." I said.

"Jazelle you need to get out of the house and live a little. You always crying that your life is boring, but you don't do anything to change it. Get out and have some damn fun." Karli said smacking her lips

"I don't know Karli, you know that I have to clear it with Antonio first and check with my mama and see if she will keep the girls overnight." I said trying to get out of going out like I did every time she asked me to go out with her. My mama was already gonna keep the kids for the whole weekend.

"Come on Jazelle, please. I don't want to go by myself. You know that you are my only friend." Karli whined.

"Ugh, you get on my nerves. Let me talk to Tony and I'll call you back in a little bit and let you know." I said

"Ok friend. You better say yes though." Karli said and hung up the phone.

Truth is, she was right. My life was soooo boring. Same shit day in and day out. Same damn routines. Same damn food. Same damn everything. No excitement. EVER. Not even in the bedroom. Antonio had lost his touch, and I was disappointed, to say the least. It was like we only had sex because we had to. Because it was my obligation as his wife and his obligation as my husband. Nothing about it was enjoyable.

I sat on the couch thinking about rather or not I should go out with my friend. Hell, if I did go, I most definitely didn't want to go to no damn Highlands. It was full of bad ass teenagers and ratchet bitches. The only ratchet bitch that I liked was Karli. I decided to call Karli back and tell her we could go out, just not there. I wasn't even going to ask Antonio because I knew that he wouldn't want me to go. I would just let his ass know that I was going and hope that he was ok with it.

The phone only rang once before Karli answered the phone

"So, what's it gone be bitch, you going or nah????!!!" Karli screamed into the phone. This bitch didn't even greet me.

"Yea I'ma go." I said. "But not to Highlands. Let's go to Dallas Cabaret I haven't been there in forever." Karli loved strip clubs, so I knew she'd be down with that.

"Yaaaaaas bitch," Karli said. "I'm driving cause you getting fucked up tonight. I'll pick you up at 10."

"Ok," I said. Before I hung up, I heard Karli call my name.

"What is it Karli," I said

"Bitch when I pick you up you better be cute, and not looking like somebody's granny," she laughed.

"Forget you thot," I said as I hung up the phone.

I loved Karli. We have been best friends since high school. We met freshman year at Eastern Hills High School and she had been the same honest, tell it like it is, always got my back friend that she is today. Our bond was unbreakable. We were always together and I didn't think that it would ever change. She's the one who introduced me to Antonio. They lived in the same apartment complex, and she thought we would be a 'great fit' which we were...... Until now.

"Jazelle? Are you okay baby?" I heard Antonio speaking. Ugh, I thought his ass was sleep. I thought as I snapped back to the present.

"Yes, babe I'm ok," I said.

"I just got off the phone with Karli's crazy ass." I laughed.

"We're going to go out tonight, so I need to get dressed. I'll order you some pizza, and wings and turn the game on for you. Cool?" I was hoping he would be ok with it. I never went out so what harm could one night of fun cause.

"Yea baby that's cool. You go and enjoy yourself and be safe. Don't get into any trouble with Karli because we both know how she is. Or do you need me to come with y'all?"

"I will," I said ignoring him trying to tag along and dogging out my friend. I needed this night, and my clingy husband was not going to ruin it. I know that most women wanted their men to spend all of their free time with them, but let me be the first to tell you ladies, that shit is exhausting. On top of that, he wanted me with him all the time, but he wasn't even fucking on me. I mean at least give me some dick if you gone be in my face all damn day.

I walked out of the living room leaving Antonio on the couch by himself and headed upstairs to our bedroom thinking of what I was going to wear. I can't believe Karli said I be looking like somebody's granny. I wasn't the fly-est bitch, but I wasn't no damn granny either. I was a 5'4, dark skinned beauty. I had cat-like bedroom eyes that were the color of honey, they sparkled in the light and they were piercing and intense. I was always told that my eyes were my most beautiful asset. I had thick pouty, kissable lips that were a perfect mixture of pink and brown. At 175 pounds I had a little cushion for the pushing, and my husband used to love it.

I stood in my walk-in closet and stared at my clothes that I never really got to wear since I didn't go anywhere until I found something to wear for the night. I decided on a black lace jumpsuit that I ordered from Fashion Nova. It was sexy and risky and fit my body like a glove. It was different than what you would usually catch me in. I was always in some jeans and a t-shirt. I had never worn it before because I knew that Antonio would have a conniption fit the moment that he sat me in it. It was an impulse buy, but tonight I was going to wear the hell out of this outfit and Tony was just going to have to deal with it. I paired it with black and gold strappy five-inch stilettos that I got from J'Dior Royalities Co. These shoes were made for sitting only but they were too cute for me not to rock at least once. It was only 8:00 pm, so I had about two hours to get dressed. I placed my outfit on our King-sized bed with some gold earrings and some gold bangles and headed to the bathroom to wash up.

I decided to opt for a bubble bath instead of a shower. We had a big beautiful jetted Jacuzzi tub that I was in love with. It was my favorite part of our master bathroom. I ran my water as hot as I could get it and added my favorite bubble bath 'warm vanilla sugar' by bath and body works. I lathered my towel and bathed my body starting at my neck and working my way down to my toes. Bubble baths always relaxed me and allowed me some much-needed alone time. After 20 minutes I finally decided to turn on the shower head and rinse my body of the excess soap.

I detached the shower head, so I could get to my hard to reach spots. I let the water hit my body lower and lower until I reached my pussy.

Once that water was hitting my clit like I did something to it, I was zoned out. I couldn't move that shower head if I wanted to. The feeling was so intense, but I didn't want it to end. My mouth fell open as I felt that all too familiar tingle in my belly, and I knew I was about to cum. After a few more seconds, my body exploded so hard that I couldn't tell you where the shower water began or where the cum that flowed out of me ended.

"*Whew!*" I said to myself.

I definitely need that. Antonio and I weren't not having sex like we used to. Not since the birth of our second daughter who was already five years old. We had sex probably every two to three weeks. So yes, that shower head gave me life, killed me and then brought me back.

Once I got out of the shower, I dried off and began putting lotion all over my body with my warm vanilla sugar body lotion.

"Damn this smell good." I thought.

I put on my Black lace panties and matching bra as I stared at myself in my full-length mirror. I admired my imperfections. I was a baddie, and no one could tell me different. My ass sat right, and my titties were still nice plump, and perky even after two kids. I knew that I couldn't be the reason for the lack of intimacy in me and Antonio's relationship.

I sat at my vanity and applied my makeup to perfection. I stayed in Sephora buying up all the Fenty products I could afford. I put on my clothes, called Pizza Hut and headed to the living room to wait on Karli's call.

When I got to the living room, Antonio jumped up from his seat like his ass was on fire.

"Where the fuck you think you going dressed like that? You need to go back to the room and change out of that hoe wear!!" He yelled.

I couldn't believe this jerk just said that to me. He had never spoken to me like that before. I also had never worn anything so revealing before. I was not having him talk to me like I was some child. Not happening. He had two kids, but neither one of them were me. Before I could go off on his ass, Karli called me.

"I'm outside Bitch," she said when I answered the phone.

"Alright, I will be outside in just one minute" I said to her before hanging up the phone. I calmed myself as I turned my attention back to my husband.

"Look, Antonio, I love you, baby, calm down. It's just a girl's night out. You know that I'm just going out with Karli and that you have nothing to worry about. I hardly ever get to go out with my friend babe, so just let me enjoy my night, and I'll be coming back home to you," I said as I kissed him and headed out the door before he had a chance to say anything back to me.

Once I hopped in the car with Karli, I knew that she could tell I was annoyed.

"Girl why your face look so stank?" Karli asked.

"Girl don't even worry about it. Just Antonio working my nerves again," I replied. She rolled her eyes at me, stepped on the gas and sped out of my neighborhood.

I loved my city. Ft. Worth, Texas was my hood. I was born and raised in the Funk. But shit just wasn't popping like it used to. These niggas stayed robbing and shooting innocent people, and all of the clubs were trash. Karli let it be known that she never partied in Ft Worth. We were heading down I35 towards Dallas. We pulled up to Dallas Cabaret, and the parking lot was packed. It took us a minute to find a parking spot. Once we parked, I pulled the mirror on the sun visor down to check my makeup and to make sure that I was still flawless.

"Ok Jazelle, I see you looking like a sex doll tonight. I'm surprised Antonio let you out the house looking like you looking." Karli said.

"Girl he sure didn't want to," I laughed. "He called it hoe wear."

"Hell, I'll take this over your granny attire any day. Come on let's go get in line," she said.

The line was long as hell, we waited a good 40 minutes before it was our turn for the bouncer to check our ID's. My feet were already aggravated in these shoes and the night had barely even started. The bouncer looked us both up and down and told us that we needed to have escorts in order to get into the strip club.

"What the fuck!!" Karli yelled in regular Karli fashion. "Since when do we need escorts to get in the damn strip club!? We just stood out here in this line for 40 damn minutes. You got me fucked up with yo dingy musty bad built ass. You look unsanitary as fuck to me. Somebody gone let me up in this motherfucking club." She screamed to the bouncer.

He looked at Karli like she was crazy and turned to the next person in line completely ignoring her question. I felt like it was a valid question and I wanted an answer too.

I was absolutely pissed because of this big, ugly, rude ass bouncer; doorman; security. Whatever the hell you call the people that stood at the door of the clubs talking shit.

I really wanted to hit Dallas Cabaret tonight. It was one of the hottest strip clubs in Dallas, and I haven't been in forever. I didn't want to go back to the house just to watch boring ass western movies with Tony.

I turned around to walk back to the car with my head in my phone looking for something else that would be popping tonight, as I turned, I bumped into something big strong and solid. I looked up to see that it wasn't a wall that I bumped into, but a man and OH MY GAWD was he a work of art. He was about 6 foot 4 and black as night. He had straight pearly white teeth and big wide doe-like eyes. He smelled so good, I just wanted to lay my head on his chest and sniff him. That would have been creepy, so I decided against it. He had the thickest healthiest fullest beard that I had ever seen, and it outlined his thick lips perfectly. Yes, I was definitely lusting after this man right now. He reminded me of Kofi Siriboe, but bigger and taller. I was mesmerized by the sight of him and turned on by the thoughts of what I could do to him. Gawwd this man was gorgeous.

"Where you headed to pretty? Why are you leaving so early? He said to me

I was so caught up in my thoughts that I couldn't even answer him. I knew what I wanted to say, but the words just would not escape my lips.

"They won't let us in the damn club cause we ain't got no escort! Ain't that some shit??" Karli said.

I was so caught up that I forgot her loud mouth ass was here.

"It's good baby, me and my boy will escort you both in," he said pointing to his equally sexy friend who put me in the mind of a young but much taller Larenz Tate.

"What are your names anyway?" The sexy chocolate man asked

"I I I'm Jazelle, and this is my best friend, Karli," I stuttered. Yes, he was just that fine, had me stuttering and shit.

"I'm married and I love my husband" I told myself.

"HAHA alright then Jazelle and Karli, I'm Donte, and this is Eric. After you ladies," he said pointing towards the door of the club.

We walked in the club and headed straight for the bar.

The club was too turned up. I was having an awesome time, and Karli didn't lie when she said I would be getting fucked up tonight. She was buying drink after drink and shot after shot, and I wasn't turning down anything. I was in my zone.

I expected Donte and Eric to go their separate ways once we got in the club, but they stayed with us and was enjoying the night. Karli kept trying to dance with Eric, but he kept stepping away from her each time she put her ass on him. It tickled me because Karli was such an alpha female, I'm sure she was scaring him away.

After a few more hours at the club, the DJ called last call. It was closing time and they played all the older ratchet music at the end.

"Can I have a dance pretty?" Donte said Flashing that million-dollar smile.

"I'm sorry, but I don't dance Donte," I said loudly trying to make sure he heard me over the music.

"Bitch you better pop that ass for a real nigga, it's just a dance," Karli whispered

This bitch was nosey. She needed to be worried about why Eric been running from her ass all night. I shrugged it off and grabbed Donte's hand and headed to the dance floor. I might as well have the best time that I could have while I was out and one dance never hurt anybody.

She Twerkin by Cash out was on, and that was my

shit!!!

See me grabbin' on my tooly

She told me smack her on the booty

She say I got too many hoes

She say I got too many shows

But she twerking

But she twerking

But she twerking

But she twerking

But she twerking

But she twerking

But she twerking

But she twerking

This song always brought out my inner stripper. When we got to the dance floor, I started grinding on his fine ass. I was swaying my thick hips and popping my ass like I didn't have a husband at home.

I could feel his hands snaking all over my body, touching the most intimate parts of me. He was grabbing ass, hips, and thighs, and I just continued popping my ass on him like he was my man. I could feel his dick getting hard on my ass, and it seemed to me that he was working with a monster. But that was none of my business. I had to get away from this man. I've never been turned on by a man other than my husband, but the way Donte was grabbing me made me feel things I've have yet to feel in places that have been unexplored and untouched for far too long. I tried to walk away from him, but he grabbed me by my waist and pulled me closer to him. He leaned down and placed his face in the crook of my neck and held me in the middle of the dance floor.

"I got to have you," he whispered in my ear. His hot breath felt so good against my skin. I was melting underneath him

"I'm married," I said.

"What does that have to do with me?" he replied with a smile.

I have to get away from him," I thought.

"Come on bitch, let's go," Karli said as she approached us on the dance floor.

I was grateful because I was drunk as fuck and ready to hit the sheets.

We started towards the exit, but Donte blocked me.

"How about you give me your number pretty," he said.

"I can't Donte, I already told you that I'm married," I said yet again trying to avoid what I knew I really wanted.

I know I said I wanted something new, but damn I haven't really had time to dwell on the pros and cons yet. I can't be making rash decisions and giving any and every-one my number. I had to really think this out. Did I really want to give someone else something that only my husband has had the pleasure of experiencing? Something that was sacred, and not to be shared with anyone else. Did I want to give myself to this man that I had only known for a few hours?

I know that he just asked for my number, but there is so much more that comes with that. He's asking for my number now, but he'll be asking for what's between my legs next.

Next thing I know I hear Karli blurting out my number to him. This bitch sure was adamant about me talking to another nigga. What was that about??

Karli Washington

Jazelle is my girl. We've been friends for a long time, and I loved her like a sister. But she is ungrateful as fuck. I mean, she has a man that is down for her and loves her more than anything. Yet she complains about him being boring and clingy. I wish I had a clingy boring ass man like Antonio. All I got was hit it and quit its, one-night stands, and other women's men. I introduced Antonio and Jazelle when we were 18 years old, and they have been together ever since. I made a fucking mistake because I definitely didn't think that they were going to get married and have kids. When I saw in the very beginning how he treated her, I wanted that for myself, but Antonio is faithful, and he wants Jazelle and only Jazelle.

I know I'm wrong for lusting after my best friend's husband, but I was jealous, and I just know that I can treat him so much better than she can.

So, when I saw Donte at the club, I knew that I had to convince her to talk to him. It was the only way that I could get what I wanted. I gave Donte Jazelle's number because she was acting like she was so in love with Antonio, and didn't want to give it out. But she wasn't about to fuck up my plan. I wanted Antonio, even if that meant sacrificing my relationship with Jazelle. What can I say, I'm a selfish ass bitch. I knew that, and everyone who knew me knew that too.

"Thank you, Karli," Donte said after I gave him her number.

He was smiling at me kind of hard, but we were all drunk, and all night his eyes and actions showed me that he wanted Jazelle. So, I pushed that thought of maybe to the back of my mind.

"No problem handsome, you just make sure you use it," I smiled flashing my bottom grill at him. If he didn't want Jazelle, I would probably want him for myself also. Damn, everybody wanted her.

After I dropped Jazelle off at her house, I decided to hit up one of my little dips. I was tipsy and horny, and I needed some dick.

Javier was a married man like all of the other men that I dealt with, but he always made sure to break me off when I needed it. He never said no and always showed up on time. What he said to get away from his wife, I don't know, and I don't care.

His wife, Emily is my personal trainer. One day she had us do a session at her house, and her fine ass husband was there. He kept coming in and out of the workout room bringing water and asking if we needed anything. If you ask me, I think he was just trying to be seen, but what do I know. Javier was tall and built, I guess compliments of his wife, and he reminded me of Rio from Good Girls. Sexy with a hint of danger. He was exactly how I liked my men, married and fine as fuck.

Once our session was over my trainer had another client, so she stayed in the workout room while I walked myself out. As I was walking out, her next client was coming in. She was a beautiful dark-skinned woman with a blunt cut bob. She walked past me and waved as she sashayed her way to the workout room. She seemed so confident. A confidence that was different from my confidence. I was confident only about stealing the next bitch's man. She seemed confident about life. That's a feeling that I had always wanted to have.

Anyway, when I got to my car, I saw Javier jogging to my car with the biggest smile on his face.

"What's up Ms. Karli, take my number," he said handing me a piece of paper with his number on it. "Call me when you want a real workout."

"What's up with the paper though?" I said.

"What is this? The 90's."

"I'm old school baby," he replied.

I smirked at him, took the paper out of his hand, hopped in my car and burnt off. I didn't even need to say anything. What's understood never needed to be explained.

Javier agreed to meet me at the Hyatt in Downtown

Ft. Worth. He never came to my house, and I never went to his. Well, at least not to get dicked down. I mean, I had a little respect.

I rushed to get there to freshen up before he came because the club had me smelling like cigarette and weed smoke, I had to be fresh for our man. I got in the shower and lathered my body in the hotel room soap. I made sure to hit all my hotspots twice.

As soon as I hopped out the shower, I heard a knock on the hotel room door. I wrapped a towel around my body before I answered the door. A smile crept across my face because I knew we were about to tear this hotel room up. Javi worked my body out better than his wife ever could. He was not lying when he told me he would give me a real workout.

"Hey mami, I see you missed daddy, " Javier smiled at me.

"Sure did baby," I giggled.

"Did you miss me?"

"All day every day," he said.

One thing that confused me about Javier was that he made it clear that he loved his wife, but he couldn't leave me alone. When we were in each other's presence, you would have thought we were together. You would have thought that he loved me. He didn't love me though, he loved this pussy, and he loved his wife. I can't even tell you why men cheat on beautiful, faithful women like Emily with women like me. Was it the thrill of doing something they knew they weren't supposed to do? Was it the thrill of the feel of new pussy? I don't know. But if he knew any better, he would make sure that he kept his wife happy because once I've had my fun, I was out.

Javier was looking too good to me, and I wanted him so bad, so I dropped my towel. He could never resist this body that I paid his wife a nice amount of money for. I seductively walked over to him and pushed him on the bed. I helped him out of his jacket and shirt. I straddled his sexy body and began kissing his neck. I pulled his shirt over his head and placed soft kisses all over his chest. I moved down to his stomach placing kisses and teasing him. He was always turned on by the way my lips felt on his skin.

He unbuckled his pants and pulled them down to his ankles. He grabbed the back of my head guiding it towards his erection. I hated when he did that, but I wasn't the type of bitch to complain. Javi had one of the biggest prettiest dicks that I have ever seen, and I loved sucking his dick. I made sure that my mouth was wet cause daddy liked it wet, warm, and sloppy. I took the head of his dick into my mouth, and I could taste the pre-cum on my tongue. I loved the way Javier tasted. I devoured him and took him all in. I could hear soft moans escaping his lips, and I could feel my juices dripping down my leg. I pulled up to the tip of his dick and used both hands to jack him while I sucked on the tip. I did that for a while so that I could catch him by surprise when I went all the down on the dick until my lips hit the base of his shaft. I held it there and let the back of my throat contract against the tip of his dick.

"FUUUUUUCCCCCCCK Karli," he moaned, which only made me go harder. He sat up and grabbed the sides of my face and preceded to fuck my face...... hard. I gently grabbed his balls and began to massage them. I let my tongue slip to the area between his balls and his butt, and the nigga went crazy.

"AHHHHHHHHHHH Karli! Shit girl, FUUUCK. I felt him getting ready to cum, so I pulled my face out of his grasp and let his dick pop out of my mouth.

"What the hell you do that for?" He damn near whined.

"SHHH baby, it's my turn," I said.

I turned around and straddled his face and leaned forward towards his dick and let his tongue send me into a frenzy. Javi sucked my pussy so hard, but so soft at the same time. He stuck his long tongue in my pussy and fucked me with it like it was a dick.

"Oh My God Baby! Oh My GOD!" I screamed. He was attacking this pussy so good that I couldn't concentrate on anything else. I grinded my pussy against his tongue and he sucked my clit in his mouth like a damn vacuum cleaner. I felt everything, the sting of the smacks to my ass and the slips of his tongue into my ass.

To me, sex was a competition, who could make who bust first, and I was not about to lose. I could feel my nut building up in my stomach, so I greedily sucked and slurped on Javi's dick until I felt him release in my mouth and I hungrily swallowed it all. I wasn't far behind him as I squirted all over his face. My pussy was leaking like a faucet, dripping nonstop. Javier looked like he was about to drown, but I wasn't having that, I reached for the condom and rolled it onto his semi-erect dick.

One thing I never did was fuck without a condom. I wasn't trying to have any babies. I was too selfish to be a mother, and I definitely wanted no ties to these men after we ended our affairs. I got on top of him and rode him like I was a jockey at the Kentucky Derby. I was so wet it sounded like I was splashing water all over him. I could feel his dick hitting my G-spot which caused me to moan out to him.

"Mmmm Javi baby, this dick is so good." I looked down at him, and his eyes were rolling to the back of his head. I knew he was on the brink of cuming.

"Come with me baby," he said. I sped up bringing my pussy to the tip of his dick and slamming it down repeatedly until I came so hard, I felt like he snatched my soul out of my body through his dick. My body was convulsing on top of his. I rolled off of him and laid beside him so that I could catch my breath.

I was so turned on because having sex with another woman's husband gave me a high like no other. I couldn't control myself. It was euphoric. It made me feel like they wanted me more than they wanted their wives and gave me a confidence like no other. Also, I loved the fact that I almost always controlled how these affairs went down. I ended them when I wanted them to end. They didn't leave me until I was ready and I loved the power it gave me.

"Damn girl, you got me wanting to ditch hanging with my boys to lay up with you all night," Javi stated pulling me from my little daydream.

"Now Javi, you know that ain't what we about baby. We fuck, and then you go home to your wife. Nothing has changed hun'. Go ahead and get your clothes on so you can go. I need to get my beauty rest."

"Aight. Bet," he basically growled at me.

I watched as he put his clothes back on piece by piece and was tempted to go for another ride on that beautiful dick of his. But like I said, it was time for Javi to go.

When Javier left, I sat in my thoughts. Most of the time I was ok with the woman that I was, but the times when

I was left alone with a wet ass and the demons that plagued my life, I wondered what was wrong with me. I wondered why I wanted things that I couldn't have, and by things, I meant men. It's a dangerous game fucking with other women's husbands, but it was addictive. It was a game that I was enjoying. And I would only stop when I was good and ready.

It was my mother's fault that I was the way that I was. She allowed her husband full access to my body, my mind, and my heart. She didn't exactly hand me over to him, but she didn't protect me either. When I told her about him sneaking in my room and having sex with me while she was working, she played me like I was a liar. She said why would her man want me when he had her to fuck every night. Shit, I wanted the answer to that same damn question. How could she sit idly by and allow me to be raped almost every night, and not do anything about it. I just can't forgive her for that.

Instead of getting mad or sad about it, I just got fucking even. She wanted to play me, so I took her man....at least I thought I did. My stepfather, Robert and I had a whole relationship. We went on dates, trips, and had plenty of sex. I was a 15-year-old little girl, and he took away my innocence. When I fell in love with him, he backed away from me. He told me that he loved my mother and not me. I begged for him to love me and to leave my mother so that we could run off together, but he would not budge. He didn't love me, and there was nothing that I could do about it.

It took me a long time to figure out that he wasn't even good enough for me. He wasn't worth the pain that he caused me. If my mother would have protected me like a mother should've, I probably wouldn't have gone through that. I would have known my worth. I probably would have been a decent person with morals and shit. I guess my mother was just as much a selfish bitch as I was. From that moment on, I decided that I would play these niggas before they played me. Even if these men did tell me they loved their wives, I wouldn't give a damn, because ever since Robert used and abused me, I didn't have any love or any fucks to give. Story of my life huh. I'm fucked up. Since nobody ever gave a fuck about Karli, I sure didn't give a fuck about anyone else.

I decided to stay the night at the hotel, it was already paid for, and I was tired and didn't feel like driving across town to my apartment. I remembered Jazelle asked me to text her when I got home. I decided to shoot her a quick text and get some rest. I had to be up by 10:30 to check out.

Karli: Hey girl, I made it. Sorry, I forgot to text you when I got here.

Jazelle: Ok I was just about to call you to girl. Goodnight.

I tossed my phone on the nightstand and drifted off.

The next morning, I woke up checked out and headed home. I wanted to shower and get cute because I had a session with Emily, my personal trainer and sister wife, and I knew our man was going to be there. I often wondered if she had any idea that her man was stepping out on her, but she was so green and naive that I doubt she thought he would ever do anything like that to her. Even if she did know I wouldn't give a fuck. We were in-laws, so she would have to get with it or get over it.

When I got home, I immediately hopped in the shower and began to lather my body with my beautiful you shower gel. The hot water massaged my body and relaxed me. I closed my eyes and fantasized about my next victim....... Antonio. I rubbed my pearl as I thought about how Antonio's lips would feel wrapped around my clit. I imagined him sucking me slowly and pinching my nipples between his fingers. The more I thought about him, the faster my fingers went over my hot button. I pictured him ramming his dick in and out of my tight pussy until we both came together. My legs stiffened, and my heart rate and my breathing speed up as I gave myself a mind-blowing orgasm. Damn, I thought to myself, I got to think about Antonio more often.

Antonio Henry

I tried not to sit up and wait on Jazelle to come home, but curiosity got the best of me. She'd been acting different lately, and I couldn't for the life of me figure out what the hell was wrong with her. I mean, I've always been good to her and treated her like a Queen, but she started making me feel like I'm giving my love to the wrong person. I fight temptation every day all out of love for my wife. All the pussy being thrown at me, and I wasn't catching nothing. More than anything, I wanted things to work out with my wife, but if she wanted to continue to push me away, she might just get what she's insinuating that she wants.

It was after 3 am, and Jazelle still hadn't brought her ass home. I was just about to call her to see if she was still alive and kicking when I heard the door chime, indicating that someone had just entered the house. I turned over to my side and pretended like I was sleeping. I could hear her little sneaky ass tiptoeing up the stairs and into the bedroom. She tried to ease into the bed with the stank of the club still seeping out of her pores.

"Baby you should shower, you still smell like the club, and it's strong as fuck," I said.

Man, she gave me the ugliest most hateful look and turned over and went to sleep without saying a word to me.

Something has got to give.

The next morning, I got up to make Jazelle breakfast in bed, I could always throw down in the kitchen, and that was one of the things that she used to love about me. I hooked her up some eggs, bacon, sausage, hash browns some biscuits and a big glass of orange juice. I was hoping we could get out of the house and spend some much-needed time together; Lord knows we needed it. We've been so disconnected, and our sex life showed it. We haven't been having sex, and when we did it was mediocre at best. That was all on me though, I was going through some things that I needed to shake back from immediately.

I walked up to the bedroom with her tray of food, and though she didn't know it, I seen her quickly tuck her phone under her pillow as if she didn't want me to know that she was on it. I ignored it and blamed it on my conscience because it had to be me.

"Hey baby, I made you some breakfast," I said.

She sat up fast as hell, hair all over her head and boogers in her eyes and still looked like the most beautiful woman in the world to me.

"Awww thanks, babe," she smiled.

"I'm starving." She grabbed the plate and quickly started to devour the meal as I sat and watched her.

"You know, I was thinking that we could spend the

day together seeing that we haven't had any alone time in such a long time," I said.

"I wish that I could baby, but I already made plans with Karli. We can spend some time together tomorrow or something." She said still stuffing her mouth with her breakfast.

I was disappointed.

I didn't like the way she had just blown me off like I was an afterthought to her. Like I wasn't important.

"Ok cool," I said.

"I'll just stay back and kick it at the house. Maybe we can watch a movie and relax whenever you get back."

"Yea Tony that'll be good," was all she said as she dug back into her food.

Every time she denied me and turned me down, I felt like shit. To tell you the truth, I was getting closer and closer to giving up on this marriage. If I really wanted to, I could hit Jazelle where it hurts, but I was a sucker for her. Karli was always eyeing me and flirting with me, but I always gave her the cold shoulder. She was fine as fuck, but she wasn't wifey material or even side bitch material. She was a hoe, and my wife's best friend so that meant she was off limits.

I laid in the bed and watched Jazelle shower and get dressed. She sure did pull out all the stops for her just to be going out with Karli. I decided to keep what I was thinking to myself. Saying anything would have just started an argument that I didn't have the strength to participate in. I decided that I could either sit here and wait for Jazelle to come back from wherever she was going, or I could go out and do my own thing. I mean what is the sense in sitting here and dwelling on the rejection from my wife, when I knew that someone, somewhere wanted me.

I sat in my office and waited until Jazelle was dressed and ready to go. Once she left, I hit up one of my gym buddies that had been asking me to hit the town with him. I always turned him down, but today, I was sending out the invitations, and hopefully, he accepted. Unfortunately, for me, he didn't answer, so I shot him a text message

Antonio: Donte, hit me up bro! I'm trying to get out of the house today!

Donte: Can't bro. I'm busy until later.

Antonio: Bet!

I tossed my phone on to the couch beside me. Now, what was I going to do? I didn't have many friends because, for the last ten years, my life revolved around Jazelle. When everyone else was out being social, I was following my wife around like a lost puppy. I couldn't help myself, everything about Jazelle was addicting. From the way she smelled to the way she laughed. Her walk, her voice, her lips, just everything. Obviously, this was still my problem. While she was out doing her, I was here alone just thinking about her.

I decided to just get up and head to Boomer Jack's in Arlington off Cooper and just have a couple of drinks by myself. It'll do me some good to get out of the house. I felt pitiful as fuck sitting around the house like I was the female and she was the cheating husband.

Once I reached my destination, I walked in and headed straight to the bar. I flagged down the bartender and ordered me a Jack and Coke and decided to text my wife since it had been a few hours since I've heard from her. I at least wanted to know that she was ok.

Antonio: What's up babe? How is your day going?

Antonio: Babe? Are you good?

Antonio: Babe??

Coming to the conclusion that she just was not going to text me back, I put my phone back in my pocket and continued to drink my Jack and coke. I was pissed off. She never used to be like this. She always answered when I called, always responded when I texted her. Now she was just leaving me hanging like I was just some stranger trying to get her attention.

"Hello, handsome," a voice from behind me said.

That voice was so sensual. I wanted to hear it again. I wanted to match that voice to a face, a face that I imagined to be beautiful.

She walked around me and sat in the seat next to me. She had on a tight-fitting red dress that draped over her shapely womanly figure so delicately. She was the color of hot chocolate with the prettiest light brown eyes. She had thick black curly hair that hung past her shoulders. Her lips were thick and beautiful and painted in red. I couldn't take my eyes off of her even if I wanted to. She was a true beauty. She ordered herself a tequila sunrise then turned to face me.

She was beautiful. Almost as beautiful as my wife. The more I looked at her, the more I noticed that she looked like Jazelle. She looked a lot like Jazelle. It was almost scary. I just sat there and stared at her. Waiting to hear that voice again.

"I'm Emily," she said reaching her hand towards me for what I'm guessing was a handshake.

"Antonio," I said grabbing her soft hand.

"What are you doing here by yourself?" I asked her.

"Waiting for my husband to finish cheating on me." She said.

I was taken aback by her honesty and her calmness about the situation.

"Why do you think he's cheating on you?" I asked her.

"Trust me," she said. Taking a sip of her drink.

"A woman knows when her man is not 100% hers. I'm not sad about it anymore, I've learned to deal."

"Damn, that's not something you should have to get used to," I said wondering if Jazelle could somehow feel if I wasn't completely hers. Or even if I would be able to feel if she was not completely mine. She made that statement so confidently that there had to be some validity in it somewhere.

"Yea, that's true," she said.

"But sometimes you just play the hand you are dealt and hopefully, when it's all said and done, and all the cards are on the table, you win."

I could tell that she was a good conversationalist just by the way she used her words and how they seemed to roll off of her tongue without a thought.

We sat and talked for a couple of hours until Boomer Jacks closed. I loved her conversation. She was so smart and articulate. Just like Jazelle. This woman sat and told me so much about her husband and their marriage that I felt like I had a front row seat and free popcorn. She was unhappy, I felt for her. All that I could offer her was friendship and a listening ear. Even though she looked like Jazelle, she was not my wife. There was no other woman for me, but Jazelle. I was still very much in love with my wife, and I knew that I could never take it there with Emily. No matter how beautiful her face was or how sensual her voice was. I walked her to her car, and we exchanged numbers. I could use a friend, and she seemed like she could be just as good of a friend as anyone else.

I made my way home with my wife on my mind. I missed her, and I wanted to fix us. Hopefully, she would be home when I got there, and we could just cuddle on the couch and watch some Netflix. When I made it home, she was not there.

Jazelle Henry

I knew I should have spent my day with my husband, working on our marriage and trying to get back close. I hated the feelings that I was having. I hated knowing that I was unhappy, even though I had a man that did everything he could to make me happy. I knew that he loved me, but even knowing that, I just couldn't keep my hot ass at home. I couldn't shake the feeling that there was something out there that I was missing out on. I felt like my marriage was a prison, and I was trapped. No freedom to do as I pleased. I just needed to figure out what was best for me at the moment. At the same time, I knew that I was being selfish and unfair to my husband, but I couldn't help it.

The morning after the club, Donte texted me and let me know that he wanted to spend some time with me and get to know me. I agreed to meet him, even after my husband made me breakfast in bed, and told me he wanted to spend time with me. Antonio was always doing sweet things like that for me.

I just feel like there is something better for me out there. Like there are things that I didn't get to experience. Ever since I was 18 years old, I've been with one man. I had his children in my early twenties, and I was a housewife. Life just didn't excite me. My life was so routine, day in and day out, my life was so predictable. I needed some spontaneity in my life. So of course, when Donte hit me up, I jumped at the chance. To me, this was new and exciting. Something completely out of the ordinary for me. I couldn't miss out on seeing what else was out there.

So, after eating the delicious breakfast my man made for me, I went to shower and get the funk of the club off of me. I can't believe I got my drunk ass in the bed without washing the cigarette smoke from my hair or wiping the makeup off of my face. I went to my walk-in closet and pulled out my clothes for the day. I got dressed in some dark blue Fashion Nova high waisted skinny jeans, my brand-new maroon silk shirt from the same brand and some maroon pumps that I got from an online boutique. Cute and simple. Antonio must have been in his office when I headed out because I didn't see him when I left. His feelings were probably hurt, but he would be alright. He could be so sensitive sometimes.

Donte had me meet him at Barcade. A bar where they have giant replicas of games like connect four and Jenga. It also had all the dope arcade games like Mrs. Pac Man and Galaga. I had never been to a place like this, so my lame ass was super excited. We played every game that they had up in this place and I kicked his ass in Mrs. Pac Man. We ate pizza and drank beer and laughed and laughed. I was having a good time. I don't remember the last time I laughed so much or had so much fun.

"Damn, how you get so good at this game?" Donte asked.

"Boy, I been teaching Mrs. Pac Man to eat balls since I can remember. What? You didn't think that I would be that good huh? You thought you was going to bring me here and whoop my ass."

"On some real shit I did," he laughed.

"But you schooled me though. You got it."

Donte and I talked about everything under the sun. He told me about his life, and I told him about my life and my husband. I was kind of embarrassed to tell him that my husband didn't do too much wrong and that there was really no reason to be stepping outside of my marriage other than my own insecurities. He understood where I was coming from and that made me feel even more comfortable with him. Antonio kept texting me, but my guilty conscience wouldn't allow me to text him back. I mean what was I going to say? Oh, yea babe, I'm having a good time cheating on you. So, I just ignored him. I would deal with him when I got home.

After we left Barcade, Donte asked me to follow him to a hotel so that we could talk a little more in private. My body automatically tensed up. I know I said I wanted something new and different, but he was moving too fast for me. I needed things to go at my pace, but that would be just another excuse for me to pass up on the things that I said I wanted. How was I going to find out who I was outside of Antonio if I've never been outside of Antonio? I took my phone out to text my best friend Karli to see what advice she would give me.

Jazelle: What are you doing?

Karli: Just leaving my workout. What's up?

Jazelle: Donte, the guy from the club last night, asked me to meet him at a hotel to talk. What should I do? Should I go?

Karli: Yesssss Bitch!!! Go!! Have fun! And get some dick!!! Lol.

Jazelle: OMG! I will not be getting any dick. But I will go and talk to him. Ttyl.

Karli: Let me know all of the details!

Karli had never been one to give sound advice. Secretly I was hoping she would tell me to go with him. I put the phone in my cup holder and waited for Donte to pull out of the parking lot so that I could follow him. All that I was thinking in my head was that he better not try to take me to no beat up ratchet bates motel.

He pulled into the LaQuinta Inn in Arlington which was fine with me. Not too fancy and definitely not Bates Motel-ish. While he went in to get the room, I tried to park my car in the very back, I couldn't take the risk of someone me or Antonio knew spotting my car. I walked into the lobby and took a seat on one of those hard ass chairs they had and waited on Donte to finish up.

Once he was done, we went up to the 3rd floor where the room was located. When we got in the room, I immediately took my shoes off. Pumps to an arcade was not the best decision, and my feet were aggravated.

We sat on the bed, and he grabbed my feet into his lap.

"So why are we here?" I asked.

"What did you want to talk to me about in private?"

"Why are you acting all paranoid pretty? I'm just trying to get to know you. I want to know everything there is about you. I even want to know the simple shit like your favorite color and your favorite food. Don't be scared of me Jazelle," He stated.

"I guess I'm just nervous. Like I told you before, I've never been this close to another man so it will take some getting used to. Don't think that I don't want to get to know you or anything, I just have to move at a slower pace," I said.

"I get that. We can go however fast or slow you feel comfortable with. I'm not here to rush you or to even push you into anything. You seem like a smart, kind, loyal woman. So, I can see why you're holding back a little bit. But you have nothing to worry about with me. I'll be your peace and your piece if you let me.

I just nodded my head as he continued to massage my feet. Let me tell you, he must have some magic in those fingers because this was the best foot massage I ever had. I just laid back on my back, closed my eyes and imagined him touching me in other places with those magic fingers. His touch was almost addicting. His hands moved slowly and methodically from my feet to my ankles, to my calves all the way up until he reached my thighs.

"Take these pants off so I can give you a proper massage. I've been told that I should have been a masseur a few times in my life," he said

All I'm thinking in my head is "OMG this man is going to try and rub on my booty. Why else does he want me to take my pants off? Lord just let this man give me a regular massage and not try to dip his fingers in my honey pot because I might not be able to control myself and bust it open for a stranger in a LaQuinta Inn.

But like a woman under a spell, I just slide my pants off like he asked me to. Thank god I wore some cute panties.

He rubbed my body like he knew every curve. Like he had been here before. He touched me like he had been wanting to touch me his whole life, and I wanted, no I needed more.

I allowed him to pull my shirt over my head. He reached behind me to unclasp my bra and then turned me over onto my stomach. He slid my panties off of me so slowly, almost as if he was waiting on me to protest, and started to massage my ass. My body went stiff, and my breath halted.

"You want me to stop?" He asked.

I just shook my head no because, at this point, I could not speak a word. I was too much in my head, and I was anticipating the next move that he was going to make. He spread my ass cheeks apart and bit both of them as he ran his fingers up and down my pussy. He had my pussy so wet that there was a small puddle forming underneath me on the bed.

He kissed my plump ass a few more times and continued to move down until his kisses resulted in his lips being wrapped around my clit.

When he put his mouth on my pussy, I couldn't handle it. He had me moaning and groaning so loud that I was embarrassed. The way his tongue felt in my pussy was more addicting than his touch. My body screamed out in pleasure as he explored me with his mouth. He was eating my pussy from the back and doing it very well might I add. At that moment, I knew. I knew that things between Antonio and I would never be the same. I knew that whatever Donte asked of me that I would give it to him, as long as he always touched me like this, he could have everything I owned. Donte ate my pussy like he was an inmate on death row, and this was his last meal. I arched my back to give him better access. He spread my lips with his thumb and index finger and sucked that nut right up out of me

"DONTE IM CUMMING BABY. IM CUMMING." I screamed.

"That's right pretty, give me that nut," he groaned into my pussy.

After I came, he just sat up and sat beside me on the bed. I was sure that he was going to give me a side of dick with this bomb ass head he just gave me, but Donte had other plans.

"Let's watch a movie. What kind of movies you like?" He asked.

"Ummm anything is cool. I'm going to the restroom. Go ahead and put a movie on," I said feeling kind of pissed off that he just basically teased the fuck out of me.

I went into the restroom and grabbed a towel to clean the mess that he made between my legs. I looked at myself and the mirror and felt a tinge of guilt. My husband probably somewhere worried about me, and I'm up in here getting my pussy devoured by fine ass, Donte. It was probably better that he stopped when he did. I was already becoming a fiend for Donte.

Donte Abraham

I knew exactly who Jazelle was when I laid eyes on her beautiful ass outside of the club. I had been waiting on the opportunity to meet her and work my magic on her. I met her husband Antonio at the gym about a year back, and all this nigga could talk about was Jazelle. How beautiful she was, how smart she was. He said everything about her was perfect, and I wanted to find out if what he was saying had any truth to it. He made his life seem so perfect, always bragging about the good things going for him. While I was stuck at home with a bitch for a wife, no damn job, and using my friend's buddy pass to get in the gym. I was dead ass broke, and the only way I got this hotel room was cause a nigga had a Groupon.

I figured if Jazelle made Antonio's life so great, then surely, she could do the same for me. I was determined to take this nigga's life one way or another. I was starting with his wife. I had no intention of completely taking her away from him, but I needed her to elevate myself. My parents always told me that a man wasn't shit until he found a good woman to stand at his side. Jazelle would be that good woman for me for as long as I needed her to.

"I can't believe that we just did that," Jazelle said pulling me out of my head. I hadn't even given her the dick yet, just a little tongue action and I could tell her body needed what I gave her. She was backed up, and I gave her a release. It was part of a greater plan. Just give her a little at a time.

"Believe it, baby. I plan on doing it over and over and over if you let me. I ain't never met anybody like you Jazelle. I'm trying to get to know everything about you. I want to know you inside and out. You gone let me do that baby?" I said.

I was laying it on thick, and I had to reiterate the fact that I wanted to get to know her so that she would be willing to spend time with me. I had to do all of this in order for her to fall in love with me like I wanted, shit, like I needed her to. Don't get me wrong, Jazelle was cool people. I liked being around her, and I liked the aura she put off. Shit, I liked her way more than I liked my wife. But I had a goal in mind, and Jazelle was just a casualty of my own twisted war.

She just sighed. I could tell that she was feeling guilty about being with me and letting me suck on that pussy. That wasn't a good sign. Obviously, this tongue didn't pull her all the way in yet. I still had work to do. But I was determined. I wanted every good thing that came to Antonio by way of her. She was the key to my happiness. If I wanted his life, then I had to have her.

My ugly ass wife would never work two full time jobs just to help put me through college. That bitch wouldn't even make me a damn sandwich if I begged her to.

Mya, my wife, didn't like me, and I hated her. She lied and tricked me into marrying her. The beginning of our relationship was good. We had good vibes together, and I thought we could really be something. Turns out, her stank ass was cheating on me with every damn body. She told me that she was pregnant with my baby so I married her. I felt like it was the right thing to do. If you knock a woman up, then you marry her and make an honest woman out of her. That's what my father instilled in my head growing up. I could forgive her for cheating, but I couldn't forgive her for putting a baby on me that clearly wasn't mine.

I knew that baby wasn't mine because I'm dark skinned, Mya is dark skinned and the baby was damn near white. We didn't need Maury telling me "YOU ARE NOT THE FATHER" for me to know the truth. She'd gotten pregnant by some white dude she had a one-night stand with. I was fucked up about that baby not being mine at first because I was so excited about being a father. My family was excited too and we were all shocked when that baby came out looking nothing like me. I wanted to divorce Mya so bad, but I couldn't. She was the one who made the money and basically took care of me. If I left her, then I wouldn't have nowhere to go.

That's why I needed Jazelle. A woman like her wouldn't do anything but elevate me. Mentally, financially and spiritually. For these reasons, I couldn't even let Jazelle know that I was married. I had to have her believe that I would be for her and only for her. That everything she was missing in Antonio she would find in me. I know the way that I'm going about this is wrong, but if Antonio wasn't always throwing his beautiful wife in my face, I wouldn't even know about her to want her.

I sat in the room for a couple of hours after my new bae left. Despite the circumstances I actually really loved being around her and hated that I had to go home to Mya's funky ass.

When I returned home, Mya was dressed and ready to go to work. She worked overnight as a RN at Baylor of Ft. Worth. I was happy she was leaving, but I didn't want to watch her son, Donte Jr. Yes, she named the damn baby after me, trifling ass. Watching DJ as I called him was how I paid for my stay here. That and dicking Mya down whenever she forced me to because believe me, I was not a willing participant. I hated having sex with her. I couldn't even stay hard half of the time. That's how much I hated that bitch. I had to have some type of connection or at least like the person a little bit in order to want to have sex with them.

But this was my life now. I was pitiful. A loser. I had to make sure I hid all that I was from Jazelle. I'm sure that if she knew I was a broke bum nigga, she wouldn't be dealing with me at all. I had to be more like Antonio. And since she told me all the things that she didn't like about her husband, and all the things that she loved about him. I knew exactly who and what I needed to portray myself as.

Today I was already going to start making some changes in my life. Just her presence in my life alone was already motivating me to want to do better. Since I've always loved to cook and I was very, very good at it, I always wanted to be a chef. I got on Mya's MacBook and started to look up culinary courses. They were crazy expensive, and I almost gave up hope until I came across a culinary course at ICDC college. It was affordable, and it said that I could qualify for grants because I was unemployed. I put in my online application and crossed my fingers that things would work out in my favor.

As I settled on the couch to watch a little TV, I heard DJ crying. He had finally woken up from his nap. As much as I hated his mother, I couldn't see myself being mean to a kid. I always treated him well and took care of him as if he were mine. It's not his fault his mama was a nasty trash bag bitch that went around lying about who her baby father was. I picked him up, fed him some homemade macaroni that I had made the night before, bathed him in his Lavender baby wash, then put on some cartoon called PJ Masks for him to watch. We watched TV for hours while I played on my phone and texted back and forth with Jazelle. Finally, we fell asleep on the couch.

***

"WHY THE FUCK IS MY BABY IN A PISSY ASS DIAPER?! And why are you laying your bum ass on my couch like you pay bills up in this bitch??!!" I heard Mya yell.

She scared the shit out of me. I farted loud as fuck and popped up out of my sleep confused as hell. She was standing there looking like an angry, raging bull, huffing, and puffing. The bitch was gone give herself an aneurysm straining her fucking face and brain and being angry all the time for no damn reason.

"We fell asleep Mya; he might have peed while we were sleeping. Look, you don't have to start tripping on me. It's not that big of a deal. I'll change him right now! Damn!" I said.

"You should have done it already Donte. You know what? I'm tired of your ass! Your ass ain't good for nothing! You already don't have a job, and you can't even do the only thing I ask of you. I'm the one who works and make money to take care of this family while you sit around and do nothing all damn day. All I ask is that you take care of our son when I'm working. You get on my fucking nerves. Where the fuck was you at all damn day yesterday? I know your lazy ass wasn't out looking for a damn job!" She screamed. Looking even more crazy than she did before.

This woman, if I could call her that, always spoke to me this way. Always emasculated, and disrespected me. She made me feel like I was nothing. Nothing I ever did was good enough for her. She acted like I was the one who brought a side baby into this relationship. All I could think about right now was the fact that I knew Jazelle would never speak to Antonio like this, and I knew she would never speak to me like this. She was just so much better than Mya in every way. Now I knew that the decision I was making, no matter how fucked it was towards Jazelle and Antonio, it was the best decision for me.

"Mya, what the fuck are you talking about our family and our son? We are not a family. I'm just here because I have nowhere else to go right now, and you allow me to stay so that you can use me as your in-house babysitter. Stop lying to yourself, he is not my son, we both know that. What I was doing and where I was is none of your business. Believe me, as soon as I'm able to, I will be out of your house, and your life. You won't have to be tired of me anymore, and you can fuck up the next man's life." I said as I walked out of the house.

It was 10 o'clock in the morning, and I didn't know where the hell I was going, but I definitely had to get the hell away from that crazy bitch.

Karli Washington

6 Months Later

A few months back, I went to Boomer Jacks with one of my men to have some drinks. While I was there, I seen my personal trainer, Emily and my best friend's husband Antonio sitting together at the bar. They sat there for hours all cozy and shit talking and laughing. I was pissed off for two reasons. One, this nigga was cheating on my best-friend with a bitch that kind of looked like her out in the open like he didn't have a care in the fucking world. Two, I was pissed at the fact that he wasn't cheating with me. I mean at least I had just as much to lose as he did. I didn't want to lose Jazelle just as much as he didn't so it would have been between just me and him, but he wouldn't give me the time of day. I had been throwing hints at him when Jazelle would leave him and I alone in a room together, but he was not interested in anything that I had to offer. I was trying to shoot my shot and he was blocking everything that I threw up.

I couldn't believe this bitch Emily either. I thought she was a naive lame bitch, but she was playing Javier just as good, if not better than he was playing her. I wondered what it was about her that made Antonio step out on Jazelle; besides the fact that they looked alike. I guess it really didn't matter because the deed was done.

After the day that I saw them at Boomer Jacks, I started following them both just to see what kind of relationship they had and if I could benefit from their actions.

Jazelle told me that Antonio hadn't been wanting to spend as much time with her as he used to, which she was happy about. It freed her up to spend time with Donte's fine ass.

It seemed to me that Emily and Antonio were in a whole relationship. I've followed them to many hotels and restaurants these past few months.

Emily spending all of her time with Antonio freed Javier up a lot for me. But he was too available now, and the thrill was no longer there. Quite frankly, I was getting bored with him, and I needed someone new.

Right now, I was on my way to chill with Jazelle at her house. I wasn't going to tell her about what I found out about her husband. Not yet anyway. This was my little secret.

***

I pulled my car into Jazelle's driveway and just sat there for a minute. I had so much shit on my mind that sometimes I just had to sit and gather myself. My mother, Dara, and her husband Robert were the two people that mostly plagues my thoughts. I hadn't seen them in almost three years. For good reason too. Every time I would speak to my mother, she would bring up the Robert situation, and call me all kinds of bitches and hoes. She said I tried to steal her man, and she couldn't trust a stank hoe like me. But she stayed with him. That's the part that really tripped me out. She stayed with him knowing that he was sleeping with her own daughter; for years, and she placed no blame on him. All of it was my fault and according to her, I made myself too available to him.

Earlier Robert called me and told me my evil ass mother was sick, and that I needed to come see her. He didn't tell me what she was sick from or how sick she was, but I guess I would find that out when I made the time to go see her raggedy ass. I knew that going to go see her would drain the hell out of me, but at the end of the day, rather I liked her or not, the bitch was still my mama.

Shaking my head and putting those thoughts to the back of my mind, I got out of the car and rang Jazelle's doorbell. She opened the door looking beautiful as hell. She was glowing like she was the happiest she had ever been. I instantly became jealous.

I wanted to glow.

I wanted to be the happiest I had ever been.

Ugh, she got on my nerves so bad these days. She had two men who both seemed to love and care for her. I just had Javier; someone else's husband who was becoming way too attached for my liking.

"Hey best friend," she sang stepping to the side and letting me in the house.

"Hey, girl! What do you have planned for us?" I said. She just sat there looking at me all stupid and shit.

"Girl I know you heard me with yo ditzy ass! I guess all that dick you getting fucking up your brain" I said.

"Yes, I heard you. Don't worry about the dick I'm getting. Worry about the many many, many dicks that you get. Anyway, Karli, I know me, and you were supposed to hang today, but I actually made plans with Donte. I told him that you were coming over and he told me to ask if you wanted to come with us. If you do, he will have his friend Eric come as well," she said.

I thought about it and decided that I would love to get a chance to see how her and Donte interacted. I wanted to see if I could snatch him from up under her and then snatch his soul from him. I mean, Jazelle is married so what does she really need with him anyway.

Maybe I would just shift my attention from Antonio to Donte; since Antonio already seemed to be juggling two women and he was totally ignoring my advances. Donte seemed like a much easier prey, and ya girl was a predator to these niggas. Eventually, she'll end up treating him just like she treats Antonio….. Like shit. So, I was doing him a favor.

"Oh, yea! I would love to get to know Eric," I lied.

"Let's roll."

Donte Abraham

These past six months have been everything that I thought they would be with Jazelle. She was showing me things that I never thought I would see. Telling me things that I never thought I would hear. I was loving it. She helped me apply for loans and grants for culinary school, and she let me know that she would be there for everything that I needed. I had already started classes a few months ago, and everything was going well. This is what I meant when I said I needed her to help me better my life. Next, I'm going to ask her to help me fix my credit, which was in the low 400's. I couldn't even get a damn prepaid Rush Card in my name. I was going to milk her for all that she was worth in any way I could. It may sound selfish and mean, but a nigga got to do what he got to do to survive. I was playing my role and playing it well. To pay her back for all the things that she had done for me, I made sure to treat her well. I gave her everything that she needed mentally. I was her shoulder to lean and cry on and her listening ear. I took her places that she had never been and always made sure to show her a good time. We still hadn't fucked yet, but tonight would be the night I got all up in them sexy ass panties she be wearing. She's been begging me for the dick, and I'm so tired of getting lock jaw from eating her pussy for hours that I decided that I'm throwing dick in Jazelle's guts all night.

I've noticed that my wife, Mya has been a little nicer to me. She's been trying to have conversations with me and go out to dinner with me. She had been cooking for me and I haven't had to watch her son in a while. I know that it's only because I'm not as available to her as I used to be. I'm always out with Jazelle, or I'm in school perfecting my craft. Maybe if she could've been this way in the beginning, things would be different for us. But it was too late for her to try to fix anything now. I was too into my thing with Jazelle to give a fuck about how Mya felt now. She would regret all the times she treated me like a bottom feeder once she sees this glow up. All courtesy of Jazelle.

I was on my way to pick up Jazelle when she texted me that Karli was going to tag along. So, I bust a U-turn and made a detour to pick Eric up. See, Karli is who I really wanted. I saw her first at the club talking shit to the bouncer before I approached them. I watched her the whole night at the club a few months back. But I had a goal in mind at the time and now that me and Jazelle were a 'thing' , I knew that it would be damn near impossible to approach her and get her alone. She was fine as hell and ratchet just like I liked them. She was loud with a sassy attitude and she didn't take nobody's shit. I could see that about her just based off her conversation with that bouncer. That shit was funny as fuck.

In the 6 months that I had been messing around with Jazelle, this would be my first time that Karli actually came around me. I convinced Jazelle to get her to come because I really wanted to see what was up with her. Like I said, this thing with Jazelle was not real, it was a means to an end.

Jazelle was my key to becoming something better than what I was, but she was not the woman for me. She was beautiful, sweet, kind, smart, and too good for me. I wouldn't know what to do with a woman like her full time. She was so soft spoken and just different from the women that I usually went for. I would only use her like I planned and live the life that Antonio makes to be so great. I wanted to wear the same type of clothes that he wore. I wanted to drive the car that he drives. I wanted to fuck the woman that he fucks; for the time being, anyway. But in the end, after I've gotten what I wanted from Jazelle, I had to have Karli.

I pulled up two houses down from Jazelle's house after scooping up Eric, and texted her that I was outside. A few seconds later her and Karli's fine ass came walking out the door towards the car.

"Get in the back nigga," I said to Eric. Dude just rolled his eyes at me like he was sweet, and got out the car.

Shit didn't surprise me; he always did sweet shit like that. Smacking his lips and rolling his eyes and shit. I didn't care though. Eric was my best friend since grade school, and if he was sweet, it didn't have shit to do with me. I'm not saying that he is.... But I ain't saying that he ain't. I'm just saying that it ain't my business.

I got out of the car just as the ladies were approaching my car. Well, my wife's car, but today, and any other day that I met up with Jazelle, it was my car. I opened the door and helped Jazelle in to the front seat of the car.

"Hey pretty," I said as I placed a kiss on her soft ass lips.

"Hey baby. I missed you" she said as she stared at me like she wanted to sop me up with a biscuit.

"I know you did," I said to her as I kissed her again and closed the door to the car.

She always looked at me like she was in love with a nigga. Maybe she was. That's exactly where I wanted her. I rounded the car and laughed to myself.

"Shit is way too easy."

Eric Sawyer

I was annoyed when Donte called me to hang with him, Jazelle, and Karli. I guess this was supposed to be like a double date, but I wasn't the least bit interested in Karli. She was one of the trashiest women I had ever laid eyes on. I've heard about her around town. About how she couldn't keep that flappy pussy to herself. I have no clue what made Donte think I wanted any parts of that. But, I agreed, because he's my best friend, and he seemed desperate for whatever reason. Jazelle, on the other hand, was everything I thought a woman should be minus the cheating shit. I didn't agree with what she and Donte were doing, but I had absolutely no room to judge anyone.

"Hey fine ass Eric," Karli all but yelled at me when she slid her ratchet ass into the back seat next to me. She looked like a fucking clown. The bitch looked like Mimi off of the 'Drew Carey Show.' Karli had a pretty face and a nice body, but she added too much of that makeup shit to her face for my liking. She had on some lime green eyeshadow shit, and bright pink lipstick. That shit had her lips looking like two busted ass hotdogs. I was disgusted.

"What's up?" I finally replied after staring at her clown face a little longer. I immediately put my head back down and started back texting on my phone with hopes that she would get the hint and leave me the fuck alone.

We pulled up to Texas De Brasil in Downtown Ft. Worth. The only thing I could think of was that this place was expensive as fuck, and I know Donte couldn't afford this restaurant. Let alone pay for him and another person. I just hope they didn't expect for me to pay for Karli's ass because that would be a quick hell to the no.

Once we found a parking spot, everyone except for Karli started to exit the vehicle. The bitch just sat in the car with her arms crossed over her chest giving me a face that I couldn't describe. It was ugly though

"What the fuck wrong with your girl?" I asked Jazelle.

"I don't know." She said while knocking on the window.

"Karli get out of the car girl! What are you doing?

"I'm waiting on Eric to open the door like a gentleman!!" she said rolling her eyes.

I was flabbergasted and appalled at the audacity of this thot thinking that someone was gone treat her like a lady. This girl done lost her damn mind. I couldn't do anything but laugh. I mean she couldn't be this stupid. With the way that I had treated her so far, she had to know that I didn't like her ass at all.

"Yo, she tripping. Is this how she acts when she gets around people she doesn't know. We on this little date by default. She acting like I'm her nigga or something.

"Eric please just open the door for her," Jazelle begged. My friend is a little special."

I was annoyed as fuck. I looked over at Donte and he just over there bent over laughing hard as hell with tears streaming down his face. He thought this shit was funny cause he liked ratchet ass bitches like Karli, and his wife, Mya. I rolled my eyes and walked back over to the car. I snatched the door open and walked the fuck off.

"Thank you, baby,'' Karli yelled further annoying me.

We walked into the restaurant and was immediately seated since it wasn't packed. I made sure to sit across from Karli because it was better than sitting next to her.

I just wanted to eat and be out. I wanted to be in the company of someone who stimulated me in ways you could only imagine. Not just stimulated my body but stimulated my mind. A couple of months ago when I went out drinking with my on again off again girlfriend, Sharise, I ran into someone. We have been kicking it super tough lately, and we were really feeling each other. Right now, I wanted to be laid up watching Netflix and talking about the future that we wanted together.

Finally, the waitress showed up, and we all ordered our food. I ordered the lamb chops, the potatoes au gratin, fish stew, and the Brazilian cheese bread. Once the food came, we proceeded to fuck this food up. Texas de Brasil was one of the best spots in the DFW. It was usually my go-to date spot because I loved the dimmed lighting. It seemed to always set the mood. Not tonight though.

Not tonight.

I was disengaged the entire time. I was texting my new bae and paying very little attention to the people around me. I did, however, catch Donte eyeing Karli quite a bit which had me confused as fuck. I was just about to ask him about it and blow up his spot when my iPhone dinged.

Bae: Hey handsome, what are you up to?

Eric: Shit nothing just hanging with some friends. Why? You missing a nigga?

Bae: I am and I want to see you tonight is that possible?

Eric: Anything is possible bae. Let me shake this company, and I'll text you when I get home.

Bae: I'll be waiting □

Now, I was desperate to get the fuck up out of here. I looked up from my phone so I could tell them that I was ready to head out. Jazelle was all over my homie, and he was making googly eyes with Karli. This bitch was supposed to be here on a date with me. Granted I've been ignoring the fuck out of her, but still, have some damn respect. Jazelle must have been blind as fuck because Ray Charles, Stevie Wonder, and every other blind person in the world could see that her Best friend and her side nigga was feeling each other.

"Aye y'all, I'm ready to shake this shit. Are y'all done cause I got to meet up with someone later," I said

"Who you meeting up with nigga? You didn't tell me that you got you a new little female friend," Donte replied

"I don't be telling you everything, my dude. But yea I got a new bae. So, what's up is we done or is we finished?" I laughed.

"UH UH, nigga you rude as fuck talking about another bitch when you supposed to be here with me. You better act like you respect a real bitch like me. I'm not about to play with your rude ass. Talking about you got a new bae. Where the fuck she at then? Her ass should be here with you so she could be bored as fuck rather than me. With your no conversation having, zesty ass," Karli said.

"First of all, who the hell you think you talking to like that? You acting like you wasn't just sitting up here eye fucking Donte like he ain't here with your friend! You want to talk about rude, but you been talking shit to me all night like we know each other. You need to calm your ratchet ass down and act like a fucking lady. I'm about tired of your fucking mouth."

Donte and Jazelle both sat there looking dumbfounded. But Karli was looking at me like she was turned on. I could tell Jazelle felt some type of way about the statement that I made about Karli eye fucking Donte because her whole mood changed. She just held her head down and wasn't speaking to anyone. I could also tell that Donte felt a way cause the nigga looked at me like he wanted to fight. It was definitely time to go. I flagged down the waitress so we could get the checks.

"Is it going to be all together or two checks?" the waitress asked.

"It's gone be three," I said.

"I'm only paying for what I ordered."

"Nigga you cheap as fu----

"SHUT YO ASS UP KARLI!!! I don't even fucking like you! Why the hell would you even expect me to do anything for your loud ghetto ass." I yelled causing the patrons surrounding us to stop and stare. I didn't give a fuck about none of them I just wanted her to close her damn mouth.

"Ummm, I'll be right back with your checks." The waitress scurried off.

This has been a bad night. Me trying to do my homie a favor ruined my mood for the night.

We all paid our checks with Jazelle paying for both her and Donte, as I figured she would and Karli and I paying for ourselves. We all walked quietly back to the car. Thank God this night was over.

***

Once Donte dropped me off at my house, I let myself in and walked into my spacious living room. 'Best Part' by H.E.R and Daniel Caesar could be heard playing softly from my Pandora app on my television. I always liked to come home to a little white noise and not just a haunting silence. I sat on my plush couch and laid my head back on the soft pillows and just thought about my life.

Everybody had secrets that they hoped would never get out. Secrets that they know could and would ruin their lives, and their reputations and destroy their very existence. I had one of those secrets. People made plenty of assumptions about me. Shit, People made assumptions about everybody. But nobody knew the true me. Nobody knew Eric.

I had done pretty well for myself financially, but it really didn't mean anything to me. I had no one to share it with. Yea there was Sharise, but we weren't together right now. Me and the new person that I was talking to were really just kicking it. We were not committed, and nothing about our relationship was exclusive. I had plenty of material things, but I had no one to love. I was lonely. I had no one to call my own, and I knew the only person that I really wanted, I would never be able to have to myself.

Ever since I was a child, my father beat the shit out of me because of who I was. I didn't live up to his standard of what a man should be. I tried. I tried to be normal. Shit, I'm still trying to be normal. But it's hard trying to be someone I'm not. It's hard hiding the biggest part of me from my friends and family. I liked Sharise, but I really only kept her around mainly for my father's benefit. He would rather me be in an unhappy relationship as long as it was with the person of his choosing.

Although I was a grown 30-year-old man, my father still beat my ass if he thought I wasn't following the path he wanted me to take. Truth is, my sexuality bothered the shit out of my father. He couldn't stand the thought of me kissing and sleeping with a man. He couldn't stand it if I acted too feminine or said something that according to him, only a woman should say.

So, he chose Sharise for me to try and take my mind off of what and who I really wanted. I really tried with her and it was kind of easy up until it was time to have sex with her. Even though she was attractive to almost anyone that laid eyes on her, she just didn't do it for me in that way. I had to force myself not to fucking vomit during sex because vaginas grossed me the fuck out. They were like open wounds that bled and stunk and I never wanted to stick my dick, tongue or a finger in those things.

Truth is,I have always been gay as far back as I could remember. With my dad being a preacher, that kind of thing went against the words he spoke to his congregation every Sunday morning. So, to keep his perfect little image, I've allowed him to control my life in the worst way. Sometimes I just wish that I could get rid of his ass and live as I pleased.

I had no idea how I would do that though. I had no idea if I could do that. I know that I couldn't just move away because my job was here and this house that I have was an investment that I was proud of. I had this house built from the ground up, and there was no way I was leaving it. I couldn't just ignore him either. My dad popped up over my house every morning and forced me to have breakfast with him. He would knock at the doors and windows for hours until I opened up and let him in. He was the most persistent man I've ever met, and I felt sorry for my mother having to deal with him on a more consistent basis. He beat her ass too, but she would never leave. She's been getting her ass beat for 32 years, and I guess she'd gotten used to it. Me, on the other hand, would never get used to that, and I knew that soon I would have to do something about it. I couldn't continue to allow him to have so much power over me, and the decisions that I made. My relationship with my mother was a tiny bit better than with my father, but it still was a shaky and tumultuous relationship. My mother knew who I was, and knew that I preferred men and not women. She accepted me when she was not in the presence of my father. But once she got around him, she would treat me just as bad as he did. I was willing to take any form of acceptance that was offered to me. I didn't really blame her for her back and forth with me because I knew that rather by fear or by choice her loyalties would always remain with my homophobic, controlling, abusive father. No longer wanting to dwell on my fucked-up life, I decided to text my bae.

Eric: Hey, I'm home. You can be on your way. I'm going to hop in the shower. The door will be open.

Bae: On my way!

I walked into my master bedroom to get my things together for my shower. My bedroom was dope as fuck. I had a big California King bed that had just enough room for me and whoever I decided to bring home to roll around in. Thick light grey plush carpet that my feet sank into with every step that I took. That was my favorite part. I felt like I was walking on clouds. The white and grey color scheme was inviting yet manly enough that my father wouldn't judge it.

After I got my towels and the clothes that I would be putting on together, I stepped into the bathroom and turned on the shower. I waited until it was warm enough to stand and hopped in. Standing under my LED light Rainfall showerhead, released so much tension in my tight wound up body. I washed my body thoroughly as I could making sure I cleaned every part of my 6-foot 4-inch frame. I knew I would be having company tonight and hygiene was important.

Just as I was getting out of the shower, I heard my company entering my bedroom. I wrapped my towel around my waist and exited the bathroom to greet him.

"Hey, baby!" Antonio greeted me.

He walked up to me and hugged my body tightly. He then placed a soft kiss on my neck. I loved the intimacy that he gave me. The light kisses, the hugs, the deep stares, and the cuddling. I even loved the conversation that he gave me. We could talk about anything from politics to aliens, and the conversation always flowed. He is the person that stimulated my mind body and soul. I loved that I was able to take off my straight man mask and just be myself.

"What's up, bae. It didn't take you long to get here," I said.

"I was already leaving the house before you texted me. I wanted to be out of there before Jazelle arrived home. She texted me and told me that she was on her way. Her mother called and told her that she was dropping off the girls early. I didn't want her asking questions about where I was going. I didn't feel like explaining myself." Antonio told me.

Ok, look, I know what y'all are thinking. But when I ran into Antonio, I didn't know who his wife was. I knew that he was married because I saw the wedding ring on his finger, but I didn't know who his wife was. I actually thought he was married to the woman that he was with at the restaurant that we met at. He was with a beautiful woman that I now know as Emily. They were just good friends, and she had become a good friend of mine also.

Anyway, as Sharise and I were walking past their table, Emily noticed Sharise and called out to her. Turns out Emily is Sharise's personal trainer. Emily invited us both to the table, and we all decided to have dinner together. Sharise and I pulled up two chairs and spent the rest of the night with Antonio and Emily. The girls were having their own little conversation and basically ignoring us. I already kind of knew Antonio from the gym. He would be there with Donte while we were working out. We hadn't spoken much when we were at the gym, but tonight me and Antonio chatted and kind of got to know each other a little more. I couldn't keep my eyes off of his lips as he spoke, but I really tried to control myself, hoping that he didn't notice. He was a beautiful man and I wanted him on another level. It was just my luck that he was into the same thing that I was into. We exchanged numbers at the end of the night and decided to get together on our own someday soon.

On the first night that we actually got together and hooked up, I noticed that his phone started ringing a lot and when I looked at his phone there was a picture of Jazelle and the name was saved under 'The Wife'. I asked him about her, and he told me her name and the current state of their relationship. I knew why their relationship was in the state that it was in, but I couldn't tell him. If I told him, then I would be putting my friend Donte in Jeopardy, and I just couldn't do that. I was conflicted because I wanted to be loyal to the both of them. I knew that when and if all this shit came out into the open, that shit was going to blow all of our lives up. In all honesty, Antonio couldn't be upset about Jazelle doing her thing while he was sneaking around town with a man.

Obviously, Antonio was undercover just like me, so we kind of used Emily as a beard for the both of us. Whenever we were in public, she was there also so no one would think that it was just Antonio and I together. She covered for us with no problems, and we both loved her for it.

"Tonight, I just want you to hold me until I fall asleep. I had a horrible night and I have a headache from over thinking my situation with my father. I just wish that I could live my life freely. Is that too much to ask?"

"No, it's not babe. We will figure something out. Stop worrying and come lay in the bed with me." Antonio replied while pulling the comforter back to climb in the bed.

I sighed and followed him to the bed and climbed in behind him. He kissed me with so much passion then held me close and tight and stroked my head until I fell asleep. I wish that I could be in his arms forever. I was addicted to the warmth of his body and the heat from his heavy breaths while he slept. I was addicted to his gentleness with me and the way he comforted me. I loved everything about him, and I couldn't help that I was on my way to falling in love with this married man. I wanted this forever. Too bad he would never be mine. At least not with Jazelle, and my father in the way.

Jazelle Henry

My life had been completely out of control lately. I was spending the majority of my time running after and falling in love with Donte, and less and less time with my husband and my children. I have put so much energy into my extra-curricular activities, that I had started neglecting my own children. This wasn't me. I had never been that type of mother or wife. But my addiction to Donte had taken a hold of my life in ways I would have never imagined. I was on a mission to get him to understand that I was the woman for him and I was willing to leave my husband just to be with him. He wasn't convinced and often brushed my thoughts to the side. I could see that I was definitely more into him than he was into me. It was as clear as day. The only time that he was somewhat interested in what I had to say was when I was helping him with school or helping him build his credit. After that night that we went out to dinner, about a month or so ago, I started to notice the distance and the disconnect between us. He started to call less and he wasn't coming around as much. I was too invested now to ever think of leaving him. He was my drug of choice and rehab was nowhere in sight for me.

Even though it had been quite some time since the dinner with Donte, Karli, and Eric but don't for one second think that at the dinner I didn't notice the way that she and Donte were eyeing each other. I was many things, but a fool wasn't one of them. I have noticed that Karli was a lot more interested in Donte than she should've been. She asked a lot of questions about things that were absolutely none of her business. I was going to keep my eyes on her because even though she was my best friend, she was sneaky and conniving. I just couldn't allow her to even think that she would be able to take Donte away from me. He was mine, and mine only and I refused to share him with anyone.

It was a rare occasion that I was home, but I was here. My children were with my mother....again, and Antonio was God knows where. I decided to clean my home because it was giving me anxiety just sitting here with all of this clutter. Ever since I've been doing me, I haven't taken the time to properly clean my home. All of that excitement that I had begged the universe for, I was now craving normalcy again.

I started in the living room, picking up toys, shoes and plates that I assumed were Tony's, and ended up in the kitchen scrubbing pots pans and countertops.

Just as I was about to take a break, I heard my phone ringing in the living room. I ran so damn fast I stubbed my big toe on the couch and almost tripped over the vacuum cleaner that I left out. I thought it was Donte, and I didn't want to miss his call. I picked up my phone off of the living room table, and it was a number that I didn't recognize. Usually, I did not answer a number that I didn't know, but I decided to answer it anyway.

"Hello."

"Hey, ummm, is this Jazelle?" The voice said.

"This is she, who's is this?"

"Hey, Jazelle this is Eric. I need to speak with you about something very important. I was hoping that we could meet up for lunch," he said.

"How did you get my number, Eric?" I asked confused as hell. The only person that we have in common is Donte, and I doubt that he would give his friend my number without asking me first.

"Look Jazelle, that's beside the point. I really need to speak to you, it's important.

"Umm ooook. When and where would you like to meet?"

"Meet me at the Jason's Deli on Cooper St at 5 o' clock. Don't be late," he said then hung up.

"Rude much," I said to myself as I headed back to the kitchen to continue cleaning.

As I was sweeping the kitchen floor, I couldn't help but to wonder what the hell Eric had to talk to me about. What could be so important that he needed to meet up with me? Why couldn't he relay the message to Donte or even just tell me over the phone. These questions continuously swam through my mind until it was time for me to get dressed for our meeting. I was a nervous wreck. I just knew that he thought he was about to tell me something bad about Donte. But he couldn't tell me anything that I didn't already know. Donte and I told each other everything for this very reason. So, no one could go back and tell us anything that the other didn't already know.

I went upstairs to my room to get dressed. I got dressed in my PINK jogging suit from PINK/Victoria Secrets and some Fenty Pumas that I just bought. I exited my room to the long hallway, and as I was walking down the stairs, I noticed Antonio sitting in his recliner in the living room.

HE WASN'T GOOD ENOUGH FOR ME

"Hey baby," I said as I walked towards him and kissed his cheek.

"Where have you been? I feel like I haven't seen you in days."

"Jazelle, where are the kids? Why are they not here with you?" Antonio asked with a perplexed look on his face and ignoring the question that I just asked him. I couldn't understand why he was asking me these questions because if he hasn't noticed, the kids were not with his ass either.

"Tony, they're with my mother. She wanted to see them. I'm not understanding what the problem is because you don't have the kids either. I hope you don't expect me to sit in the house with the kids all day every day while you let the sun beat you home most nights."

I wasn't sitting at home, but he didn't know that. He had been gone so much that he didn't even notice that I wasn't here most of the time. As far as he knew I was at home with the kids cleaning and cooking and taking care of home.

"The problem is that you're not much of a mother or a wife lately. I don't know what has gotten into you, but you need to fix that shit ASAP!! That's why I'm always gone, you're not giving me a reason to stay!!" He yelled at me.

JENAY BALDERAS

He had never yelled at me like this. This was not MY Antonio. I didn't know this man before me that was screaming and yelling and telling me he didn't want to come home to me. I was a little hurt by his words, but I shouldn't have been. He had every right to be upset with me. If he knew what I was really up to, he would die the death of a thousand men. But, if he wanted to know what had gotten into me, then he needed to ask Donte.

I felt like this conversation could go on for hours, but I had somewhere to be. This was a situation that we definitely needed to talk about, but I wasn't too pressed about fixing things with Antonio right now because I had Donte. Antonio better not piss me off because if I had to choose, he would lose.

I grabbed my keys from the bowl on the side table by the couch. I turned to Antonio and allowed the tears to gather in my lower lids for dramatic effect. Like I said, I had somewhere to be.

"I can't believe that you just spoke to me that way. You've been so distant and mean to me lately!!" I cried and walked swiftly towards the door. I snatched my purse from the coat rack next to the door and ran out the door like my name was Becky.

I needed an escape plan, and crying always worked for me. I couldn't help to laugh at my own dramatic self. I was getting too good at lying, and I really didn't know how to feel about it.

I got in my car and backed out of the driveway. I turned up the radio and heard my favorite song ever 'WEAK' but SWV. This song reminded me so much of the way that I used to feel about my husband. Now it reminded me of the way I feel about Donte. I guess I got what I was asking for. I may be losing my husband, but I was gaining what I felt to be something that was so much better. I began to sing along as I made my way over to Jason's Deli to meet Eric.

Time after time after time I've tried to fight it
But your love is strong it keeps on holding on
Resistance is down when you're around, starts fading
In my condition I don't want to be alone
'Cause my heart starts beating triple time
With thoughts of loving you on my mind
I can't figure out just what to do
When the cause and cure is you, oh
I get so weak in the knees, I can hardly speak
I lose all control and something takes over me
In a daze and it's so amazing, it's not a phase

I want you to stay with me, by my side
I swallow my pride, your love is so sweet
It knocks me right off of my feet
Can't explain why your loving makes me weak

I just continued to replay that song over and over on the Sirius radio until I arrived at my destination. It had so many feels, and this song described my feelings to the T. I parked my car in the nearest parking spot that I could and exited my vehicle. I was so nervous I could feel the butterflies in my stomach times three. The palms of my hands became sweaty as I reached for the door to enter the establishment.

I looked around to see if I could spot Eric, but I didn't see him. I walked in further towards the back of the restaurant where they had more seating and finally spotted him in a little secluded two-seater booth. I walked over to him and took a seat across from him. Once I was seated, he just stared at me, he didn't say a word, he just stared.

"Eric, what am I doing here? What do you have to tell me that you couldn't tell me over the phone?"

"I'm sorry to call you out here with such short notice, but I have something that I really need to get off of my chest," he said.

"I don't know how you're going to feel about what I'm about to say, but I couldn't continue to hide it. I want you to stay calm while we are in this restaurant. We don't need the unwanted attention."

He was stalling, and it was pissing me off.

"Just tell me what the hell you have to tell me and quit stalling please," I gritted

"Ok, so I know your husband Antonio, I have actually known him for a while. He and I work out together sometimes. But anyways, ummm, I've seen him out with a woman that I know as Emily. They are together almost every night from what she tells me. I'm only telling you this so that maybe it will make your decision between Donte and Antonio a little easier. I'm sorry that it had to be me to tell you, but I didn't want you finding out in the streets. Please forgive me if I've overstepped. I just want to see you happy with my boy. Y'all seem so good together, and I don't want you to get caught up in Antonio's shit," he said.

It was like word vomit. It just kept coming and coming, and I was still trying to comprehend everything that he just told me. My husband was cheating on me?? No! Not Antonio. He would never do anything to hurt me. He loved me too much. He's loved me since we were 18-year-old children with nothing to our names, but each other. I didn't want to believe Eric at all. I didn't realize that I was crying until Eric reached across the table and wiped the tears from my face. He looked like he felt sorry for me but I wasn't looking for pity.

With all of the things that I've done in the past few months, did I even have the right to cry. Did I have the right to be upset? Did I have the right to want to find this Emily bitch and beat her ass within an inch of her life? No. The answer is no. I didn't have the right to do none of those things, and yet here I am. I'm sitting here upset, crying and ready to fuck this bitch up.

"You said they are together almost every night? What do you mean by that?" I finally spoke up. Together where? Together doing what? Are they friends or is this something like a relationship? Are you saying that he's cheating on me?" I asked him. Secretly hoping that he didn't know what he was talking about.

"Well, Emily is a friend of mine, and she explained to me that they have dinner almost every night at different restaurants, and then meet up at a hotel. She said that they are in a relationship and have been for months. She even told me that they will be meeting up at the Benihana in Las

Colinas tonight at 9pm."

"How do I know that this is true?" I cried.

"Show up to the restaurant and see for yourself. But please don't let either of them know that I'm the one who told you. Emily told me this in confidence, and I would hate to lose her friendship over this. Again, Jazelle I'm sorry that I had to be the one to bring this to you, but I really felt like you should know what your husband was out here doing," he said

"Thank you for the information, Eric. I appreciate you telling me. But this is definitely something that I need to see with my own two eyes before I can believe it. For the last few months, I have noticed a change in him, especially towards me. But I would've never thought he could do this to me," I said while getting up to leave.

I was sad. I was hurt. I was in disbelief. I could have used this as ammunition to leave my husband and be with the man that controlled my mind and body. But this information changed the game.

I turned and headed for the front door of the restaurant still in complete shock. Even with my own indiscretions, with all the lies that I've told, I would have never thought that my husband could even look at, let alone be in a relationship with another woman. I guess karma was a cold-hearted bitch and she always came around to those deserving of her. I had to get to the bottom of this, so I'll be heading to Benihana's tonight to see what was really up.

HE WASN'T GOOD ENOUGH FOR ME

Antonio Henry

As you may already know, my secret is out. I have been running from this for as long as I could remember. I've never really been attracted to women sexually, but when I met Jazelle, that all changed. She oozed sex, so much so that she made a gay man want to be straight. I became everything that she needed me to be, a loving, supportive father and doting husband. I still remember the feeling I had when Karli first introduced me to Jazelle. It was still freshly embedded in my memory as if it was yesterday.

I remember Karli and Jazelle walking into the gated pool area of the apartment complex that Karli and I both lived in. Karli was wearing a red string bikini, and Jazelle had on a gold bikini with a sheer black cover-up tied around her waist. I watched her as she took a seat on the pool chair and pulled her wide framed sunglasses from her eyes to the top of her head. She reached into her purse and pulled out a book called 'The Coldest Winter Ever.' Then she leaned back in her chair and began to read. She looked so beautiful stretched out in that chair with her gold bikini shining bright against her chocolate skin. Her skin was illuminating from the rays of the sun. Her beautiful bright hazel eyes moving left to right as she read the words on the book that she seemed to be so in to.

She wasn't out here acting like these other females. She was reading a fucking book at a pool party like she wasn't here because she wanted to be, but because someone made her come. I couldn't take my eyes off of this beautiful, graceful, classy woman. Even though she wasn't trying to, she made me want to do things to her that I had never even thought of doing to a woman before. I watched her as she got up from the seat and walked over to the pool close to where I was. My heart palpitated at the thought of being close to her. Her walk was so delicate, it looked as if she was floating over to me. She sat on the edge of the pool with her feet submerged in the water and continued to read her book. I wanted to speak to her so bad, but I had no idea what to say or how to approach a woman. Especially not a woman like her, so I just continued to stare at her.

"Damn, why don't you just talk to her and quit staring like a creep," Karli said coming up from behind me.

"Shit, I want to, but I don't know what to say to her," I said.

"Ok dork, I'll introduce you to her, but you owe me. My best friend is one of a kind. Let me go talk to her and

bring her over here." She said as she got up to walk towards the edge of the pool to retrieve the beautiful Jazelle.

I already knew that she was one of a kind. A beauty like no other. Karli didn't have to tell me that.

I watched as Karli spoke to her. She looked over Karli's shoulder and looked me dead in my eye. She looked into my heart and my soul, or at least that's what the intensity in her stare felt like. She stood to her feet and walked over to me and stood her beautiful body in my face.

But, when she spoke to me, it was the simplest greeting, but it meant so much, and it sounded so beautiful. All she said to me was hello, but from that point on, my world revolved around Jazelle. And it had for 10 years after that. I've seemed to have gotten lost along the way.

***

Jazelle was the first and only woman that I had ever been with. Even though throughout the years, I've had those cravings for the touch of a man, I never acted on it. I had no reason to. She had been everything that I wanted and needed for so long that there was no room for anyone else. But for the last two or three years, the urges were stronger and stronger. I would watch gay porn to try and satisfy those cravings for a long while, and until I met Eric, it had been working. Now it just couldn't cut it for me anymore. I first met him at Planet Fitness while I was working out with my gym partner Donte. From the first time that I laid eyes on him, I was attracted to him, but I knew that I should never act on what I was thinking.

I had a wife at home that I knew still loved me, but with the distance between Jazelle, and I, and the fact that we weren't having sex anymore made it easier for me to gravitate towards him. I wasn't thinking with my head and my heart anymore. I was thinking with my dick.

To be honest, I was still addicted to everything Jazelle, but Eric was like the methadone to a heroin addiction. When I was with him, I had no thoughts of her. I was finally fulfilling an urge that had been buried so deep within me for so long. I felt horrible for cheating on my wife, but I felt even worse knowing that I was leading Eric on because I would never leave her for him. No matter how bad I wanted him or how much I cared for him, I had a family, a wife and two beautiful daughters that I couldn't let down. I didn't want to lead him on, but I just couldn't leave him alone. Every time I met up with him, I would tell myself that it was the last time, but it never worked out that way, I always came back for more. I knew that Eric wanted to be with me, but I couldn't live this life with him out in the open. I've hid this secret for over 15 years, and there was no way that I could let it come out now.

After Jazelle left out of the house crying, I felt bad for the things I had said to her. It was me and not her with the problem. Yes, our relationship had been on the rocks lately, but that was no reason for me to lash out at her like I did. I wanted to text her to apologize, but I felt it would be better to do it face to face.

***

I was sitting in my recliner with a Budweiser in my hand watching the Cowboy's game, when I heard my doorbell chime. I placed my beer on the side table next to me and got up from my seat to answer the door. The person on the other side of the door continued to ring my doorbell like a fucking maniac until I snatched it open and came face to face with Karli.

"Karli, Jazelle isn't here. But I'll let her know that you came by," I said attempting to close the door on her.

"I know she ain't here Tony, I actually came to see you." She said pushing her way into my home.

"The fuck you come to see me for? We don't have anything to talk about if Jazelle ain't around." I already knew how Karli was, and I wasn't about to get sucked up into her game. She had been throwing little hints and shit lately like she wanted to fuck on me. I had no intentions on exposing myself to that toxic pussy.

"Oh, but I think we do have something to talk about with your cheating ass!" She hissed at me.

My eyes got big as hell, and my stomach start to cramp. I felt like I had to shit. How the fuck did she know about Eric? I thought I had been extra careful when meeting with him. I was scared because Karli was a sneaky bitch, and I knew that she would use this against me anytime she could. Jazelle was her best friend, and I did not want her telling my secret that I had worked so hard to hide.

"Umm Karli, what are you talking about? I I I don't know what you are talking about calling me a cheater." I said shakily. Anybody could look at me and see that I was lying, so I knew that it wouldn't get past Karli's 007 ass.

"I I I Shut yo lying ass up. I hope you come up with something better than that when Jazelle finds out with yo stuttering ass.," she laughed.

"I know that you been running around town with my personal trainer Emily. You ain't slick nigga. Look, I was going to come up in here and demand that you give me some dick for my silence, but I ain't even on that anymore. You wouldn't be worth the energy it took to hide that secret. I do want you to stop seeing Emily though or I will have to get my best friend involved. Trust me Antonio. You have never seen the other side to Jazelle. She ain't all rainbows and unicorns and shit like you think. So, take heed to what the fuck I am saying. It'll be in your best interest."

What does matter to you if I stop seeing her or not? You were trying to fuck me a while ago now you so worried about me being faithful to Jazelle." I asked curiously.

"Because I'm fucking Emily's husband and the bitch is with you so much that the nigga don't know what to do with his self. He won't leave me the fuck alone, and I want her to come take him off of my hands. Besides that, I'm giving you the opportunity to do the right thing for you and your family. So, get some act right and leave Emily's ass alone." She said then turned on her heels and walked out of my house like she just didn't come in here and scare the fuck out of me.

I thought that I had really been caught. I would much rather her think that I was cheating on Jazelle with Emily than to know that I was cheating with Eric. Cheating with

Emily was much easier to come back from. But what she said was true, she was giving me a chance to get my shit right for my family. If she could find out about Emily, then she could easily find out about Eric. I couldn't chance it. I had to let him go.

The night that I met Emily at Boomer Jacks was a night that I would never forget. I met someone that I could confide my deepest darkest secrets in. She had quickly become the best friend that I had ever had. The night that Eric and I ran into each other while me and Emily were having dinner, I told her about how I felt about men, and she let me know that it was ok and that I could be myself around her. I told her about the romance budding between Eric and I, and she quickly agreed to cover for me if I needed her to. She knew the ins and out of me mentally more than my wife ever would. I could never share with Jazelle that I was gay. She would never accept me. I knew for a fact that she despised the whole undercover gay thing. She felt like if you were gay, then you needed to be gay and be honest with the person that you were sleeping with. That's why I was glad that I had Emily. There was nothing sexual between her and I, we were just really good friends that shared dark secrets.

You see, I already knew that Karli was sleeping with Emily's husband, Javier. Emily had hired a private investigator to follow him around. She knew that he was cheating, but she wanted to know with who, and the investigator found that out for her. Now that she knew, she had to figure out what to do with the information, but I had a feeling that Emily wanted to keep Karli close.

Speaking of Emily, it was almost 7:30 and time for me to start getting ready for dinner tonight. We were going to meet up at Benihana to talk about what she was going to do about her husband cheating on her.

I went upstairs to me and Jazelle's bedroom. I couldn't remember the last time I made love to my wife. I stood in the doorway and thought about the day that we moved into this house. We christened every room in this house, making love and filling up on each other's bodies. I missed that. I missed being with her, making love to her and talking to her. I just missed my wife.

I walked into my closet which was next to my wife's walk-in and pulled out my black true religion jeans and my black and white true religion shirt. I went into the bathroom and turned on the shower. Once it was hot enough, I hopped in and showered in less than 10 minutes. I got out of the shower dried off and dressed myself. I put on a little Gucci Guilty which was both Jazelle's and Eric's favorite scent on me. Jazelle always said that it made me smell like sex, whatever that meant. Once I was done, I put on my black Jordan retro 12's and headed downstairs. I grabbed my keys and my wallet and headed out of the door. I was hungry as hell and ready to see what Emily had up her sleeve.

Karli Washington

After I popped up on Antonio's ass, I hoped that he took heed to what the fuck I was telling him. I wanted him to leave that bitch Emily alone. Not so much for Jazelle, but more so for me. I was tired of Javier's ass calling and texting me all damn day. He even took it as far as showing up to my apartment, and my job. It was actually starting to scare me. This nigga was like a fatal attraction waiting to happen. I have told him that this little thing that we had going on was over plenty of times, but he wouldn't fucking listen. All of the other men that I was fucking on didn't give me problems when I let them go. Javier was a different breed though. This nigga didn't comprehend that no meant no.

So instead of popping up on Antonio with my original proposition. I decided to help myself to some damn safety instead of some dick that probably wasn't all that anyway, since Jazelle was cheating on his ass. Plus, I had already had some of Donte and honestly, I didn't need anything else right now.

The night that we all had dinner, Donte dropped Eric off first. Jazelle got a call from her mother about the girls, and she had to head home quickly, so he dropped her off next. Jazelle jumped out of the car and ran into her house without even giving me or Donte another thought. That just left Donte and I sitting two houses down from Jazelle's. It was awkward at first because it was like we couldn't read each other. We were both just sitting in his car staring out of the window not saying a word. I got fed up with him acting like he wasn't going to try to speak to me, but as soon as I placed my hand on the door handle to get out of the car, he finally spoke to me.

"So umm what are you about to do for the rest of the night, Ms. Karli? The night is still young, and I did see the way you were looking at me tonight," he stated hesitantly.

I'm sure he probably thought that there was no way that I would dip in after Jazelle, but little did he know, I was more than willing.

"Yea I was eyeing you just like you were eyeing me. Don't be trying to front like I was the only one," I said.

"Hahaha, alright so you caught me. But what's up though. You trying to get up with me tonight at my crib?"

"What about Jazelle?" I asked.

"Aint y'all all in love or whatever?"

"Nah. She may be. But I'm just doing my thing. I'm not on all that right now," he said

"So, you just stringing my friend along Donte? That's fucked up on so many levels."

"Karli, I'm not doing anything ya girl don't want me to do. Trust me. I haven't even had sex with her yet. So, are you going to roll with me or not baby?"

"Yea I'm down. Where are we going?" I asked.

He gave me an address and told me to follow him to his place. I hoped out of his car and into mine excited as hell. I was finally about to get what I wanted. And I can't say that I felt too bad about it. Maybe a little, but not much. Technically he wasn't Jazelle's man, so he was free game. I can't believe that Jazelle hasn't let this man hit the pussy yet. I mean what the fuck was she doing with him if she wasn't fucking him. But luckily for me, I was going to be able to sample him first.

I followed Donte into a pretty nice suburb in North Richland Hills and pulled up to a nice brick two-story home. I exited my car and met Donte at the front door. He fumbled with his keys a little bit before he got the door unlocked as if he were nervous. Hell, maybe he was nervous. I mean, he was about to cheat on his married girlfriend with her best friend. It didn't get any more Jerry Springer-ish than that.

This is what I needed though. I haven't felt the rush that I loved to feel when sleeping with a man that was off limits in way too long. Once he finally got the door open, the scent of a fresh laundry scented glade plug-in met my nostrils. It was strong like they were all over the house. I never met a man that took pride in the way their house smelled. It wasn't surprising, but it was different.

As I walked further into the home, I began to think that maybe this wasn't his home at all. Maybe he lived with his mother or an aunt or something. The home was decorated so beautifully, it definitely had a woman's touch. There was framed art and vases and potpourri, all things that made me feel as though this home wasn't his. I was never one to judge, it's not like I wanted anything more from him than the dick. So, if his funds didn't allow for him to have his own place, that didn't bother me at all. I walked towards the L-shaped brown, micro-fibered sectional couch in his living room and sat down with my legs crossed at the knee trying to be a classy female for once.

"Do you want a glass of wine or something while I go take a quick shower?" Donte asked me.

"I guess wine will do since I'm sure you don't have any Lime-A-Rita's in this nice ass house," I laughed and kind of tried to play off my surprise that he was offering me wine. Most times for me it was in and out. I didn't get offered anything but the dick. They didn't even put the shit on a silver platter for me.

He chuckled and walked into his spacious kitchen.

He pulled down some nice ass wine glasses and grabbed a wine bottle from a wine fridge that was built into the nice white cabinets. This shit was nice. I needed the number to the interior decorator for when I finally got me a house. I stared at him as he poured the wine into the wine glass and brought it over to me on the couch.

"Thank you," I said feeling a feeling that was foreign to me.

"You're welcome. I'll be back. I'm about to go take a shower really quick," he said and took off towards the back of the house.

It may have been a simple and thoughtless act, him pouring me a glass of wine and bringing it to me. But it felt good for someone to do something nice for me without me asking them to do it. No man has ever done anything nice to or for me without me demanding they do so. That's why I made such a big deal about Eric's rude ass not opening the car door for me. I mean, although I'm a selfish bitch most of the time, I still want to be treated like I matter sometimes. I don't want to get all sappy and shit but, I'm just saying that it made me feel good that someone did something so nice for me unprompted.

While he was showering, I decided to take a look around his big ass living room. This home was beautiful, and the teal and brown color scheme was very tasteful. I noticed pictures of a beautiful dark-skinned woman with a handsome, cute little baby boy. Maybe it was his sister and nephew or something I thought to myself. Then, I looked over at the mantle, and I saw a picture of the same beautiful woman dressed in a beautiful strapless wedding gown with Swarovski crystals all over the corset. She was standing right next to a smiling Donte who was dressed in an all-white tuxedo with a silver vest. It looked to me like he was the groom in this picture. But that couldn't be right. Jazelle didn't mention that this nigga was married. What kind of shit was this? These muthafuckas were doing way too much for me.

I didn't know if I wanted to confront him about this or not. It wasn't my place to say anything to this man, and it was kind of my thing to sleep with married men anyway.

I sat back on the couch not knowing what to think of this as I waited for Donte to return. He was obviously lying to Jazelle's gullible ass about his relationship status. This would hurt her little feelings. Suddenly, I felt justified in what I was doing. I was helping my best friend out in the end. She didn't know what to do with a man like Donte. He would ruin her, and I would be left to pick up all of the pieces.

Once he made his way back into the living room, I looked up at him, and my jaw dropped. His fine ass was standing there with his body covered in little droplets of water and a white towel wrapped around his waist. His V cuts were showing, and he was looking like a fucking snack, I no longer gave a fuck about what he was hiding from

Jazelle. I sat up straight on the couch as he walked over to me licking his lips. He kneeled down in between my legs and placed both of his hands on my knees. He snapped my legs apart which caused my short leather skirt to rise up to my hips. I was now sitting in front of him with my pussy out and my clit trying to peak through my pussy lips like an escapee.

"I wanted you from the beginning, Karli," he whispered.

Now, this nigga was just talking out of the side of his neck. That first night that we met, he was all over Jazelle, so he definitely wasn't not worried about me.

"Don't ruin the mood. Just fuck me," I moaned. The cold air hitting my pussy was turning me on, and I didn't want to talk about who wanted who.

He put his head between my legs and damn near swallowed my entire pussy. He sucked on my pussy lips and my clit at the same time. It felt so good that all I could do was open my legs wider so that he could give me more of his mouth. He pulled me closer towards him until my ass was hanging off of the edge of the couch and sucked more of me into his mouth as he shook his head side to side like a dog tearing into a steak.

The flood gates of Karli opened up, and I came all over his wife's nice fluffy area rug. My clit was jumping like criss-cross in that damn 'JUMP' video. Jazelle was really missing out. If his head was this good, I can only imagine how good the dick would be. Just as I was about to pull myself up so that my ass was no longer hanging off of the edge of the couch, Donte sat up on his knees and flipped me over onto my stomach in one swift motion.

He positioned me to where my knees were on the edge of the couch, and my body was bent over the top part of the couch. He pushed my legs apart and put his hand in the small of my back to arch my back. Once he got me positioned like he wanted me, he entered me slowly. He wasn't rough with me at all. He was stroking me so slow, and he was inside of me so deep, I could feel every vein in his dick rub against every ridge in my pussy. I felt him in my very core. I wanted him to stop or to speed up because I've never had this slow sex shit and the long deep strokes that he was giving me was a little too intimate.

I started to throw my ass back on him as fast as I could, but he would not let me gain control. He grabbed ahold of my waist tightly to slow me down and proceeded at the same slow sensual pace as before. It was agonizingly pleasurable. It was almost like he was making love to me. Or maybe this was how he fucked every woman that he slept with. Shit, why did I even care about the other women that he fucked? I don't know. What I do know is that I was cumming faster than I ever had on a dick and I was feeling every bit of what Donte was giving me.

This couldn't and wouldn't be the only time that we got together. I had to have this man on demand. After I came, my legs were like jelly, but he continued to hold my waist and give me deep passionate strokes until he came inside of me. He was so deep in my guts, I felt him throbbing inside of me. It was at that moment that I realized that we hadn't used a condom. That's what good dick did to you because using a condom was the furthest thing from my mind when he walked in here all wet and glistening.

"Fuck Donte, we didn't use a condom! I shouted

"It's cool Karli," he said. As he got up to wrap his self back in his towel.

"I'm clean. You acting like you ain't on some type of birth control."

I wasn't on birth control. I hated birth control. It always made me have cravings and increased my appetite so much that it made me gain weight. Plus, that shit had been fucking bitches up and putting them in the hospital lately. That's why up until now I made sure that every dick that I touched was wrapped up tight.

"That's not the point Donte. Ugh, let me go before your wife comes home," I stated, not realizing I that I let that little piece of information slip out.

"Wait. How do you know about that? Look, please

don't say anything to Jazelle right now. I will tell her when I'm ready," he pleaded.

I don't know why it pissed me off that he was so afraid for me to tell Jazelle, yet he brought me to this woman's house not giving a fuck if I found out or not. Her pictures were all over this house, so it was inevitable that if I had eyeballs, I would see that this nigga was married. Everybody treated Jazelle better than they treated me. They respected her more. I guess that's where most of my jealousy was about. She was just as trifling as I was though. She was cheating on her fucking husband.

I rolled my eyes and stomped over to his kitchen to get a paper towel to clean myself up a little bit. I wiped my pussy off right in his kitchen and threw the paper towel in his kitchen trash can; fuck this house. He pissed me off.

"I won't. As long as you give me some dick whenever I want it, then your little secret is safe with me." I said to him

"You could have gotten that anyway baby." He said while walking over to me and turning me around to face him.

"Look Karli my wife and I haven't been on good terms for years. Once I'm done with Culinary School, I'm leaving that bitch. So, don't even trip on her. She won't be around long."

"Mmmhmmm tell me anything. Give me your phone so that I can put my number in it. I have to get going. I have a long day ahead of me tomorrow." I said while pulling my skirt back down over my ass. Once we exchanged numbers, I walked back into the living room to get my purse. I looked over towards the mantle again at the wedding picture of what seemed to be the perfect couple. Only they weren't the perfect couple. She was caught up in a love triangle that she knew nothing about.

I recognized his wife's face from somewhere, but I couldn't remember where right at this moment. It would come to me eventually. After I picked up my purse from the couch, I headed towards the door with Donte right on my heels.

"I'ma hit you up later baby," he said.

"Drive safe."

"Ok. Have a good night," I said as I walked out of the door to my car.

I got in my car and backed out of his driveway. I was waiting on the guilt to hit me, but it didn't. I didn't feel bad about what I did. I didn't want Jazelle to find out, but I wasn't going to go to extreme lengths to keep it from her. Donte was neither one of our man. He was married and belonged to the beautiful chocolate woman on his mantle.

***

That first encounter with Donte was weeks ago. But in between then and now we fucked all over my house and his house anytime that we could. I could see myself falling for him if he wasn't already someone else's. In the time that we had spent together, he made me feel like the prettiest girl in the world. He treated me like I meant something to him. He wasn't just about the sex anymore. He was breaking down walls that I never thought anyone would ever be able to penetrate. Jazelle couldn't have him. I wanted him all to myself.

Jazelle Henry

After I left the meeting with Eric, I didn't know what to do with myself. I called Donte back to back to talk to him about this, but he didn't answer either time. He's been doing that a lot lately. I felt like I was losing both of the men that I loved. Donte was ghosting me more often than not now a days, and Antonio was cheating on me with a bitch named Emily.

I admit I have been neglecting my husband. We weren't spending any time together, and we weren't having sex at all. I should have known that it would cause him to stray. I thought that I had Antonio wrapped around my finger twice. I thought that there was no way that my doting husband would do anything to hurt me, he loved me too much. That was a fantasy though. A dream world that I was living in. Reality was what had me sitting outside of Benihana at 9:30 at night, afraid to get out of my car to see if my husband was on a date with another woman. Because then, reality would be absolutely too real, and I didn't know if I could handle it.

I sat in the car a few more minutes before I got the guts to get out and go and see this bitch that my husband was supposedly entertaining. I got out of my car to enter the restaurant not knowing rather I was going to just sit back and watch or confront him and Emily if they were indeed together.

I walked into the restaurant and took a seat at the bar. It allowed me to see all of the hibachi tables, but it was still somewhat hidden so that the patrons couldn't easily see me. I needed a drink to ease my mind and the butterflies flying around in my belly. Once the waitress noticed me, I ordered a Hot Saki. The shit was nasty as hell, but it always got the job done. The waitress handed me a little white vase and a small white shot glass. I poured myself two shots before I swiveled on the barstool to face the hibachi tables. I scanned the room for Antonio and his side bitch until I finally laid eyes on him. He was sitting alone with his head down in his phone. Suddenly, I felt my phone vibrate in my purse. I took it out to see who was calling or texting me when I saw a text from my husband.

Antonio: I was thinking about you. I love you so much

I felt foolish. Here I was, spying on my husband, trying to catch him cheating on me, and he was here alone, and he was thinking about me. I knew that I shouldn't have believed Eric. I knew my man wasn't no damn cheater. I looked down into my phone to text him back.

Jazelle: Awww babe. I love you too. Where are you?

After I texted him, I looked up at him only to see him read my text and put his phone back in his pocket. He looked sad. Or maybe guilty

Just as I was about to call his phone, I saw this very beautiful woman with mahogany skin and hazel eyes like mine. She was dressed in simple clothing, black high waisted jeans and a red wrap around shirt, but she made it look very high class with the red Louboutin's on her feet. I watched her walk over to him and kiss him on his cheek and take a seat next to my man. MY MAN!! How could he just text me and tell me that he loves me and in the same breath entertain a woman that was not me.

My heart sank in to the pit of my stomach, and I felt like I was dying inside. I did this. I felt horrible for all of the things that I was doing to my husband, and It was my fault that he was cheating on me with this beautiful woman who had some of the same features as myself. How could I compete with an obvious better version of me? She was giving my man something that I wasn't. Her time and her attention and judging by the way she was looking and smiling at him, her love.

For their whole entire date, I watched them interact. I watched them as they laughed and giggled and touched hands. I watched them as they shared their meal and ate from each other's plates. They looked as if they had known each other forever. I was jealous, angry, and hurt. All of the other thing's women felt when they found out that their husbands were cheating on them. I was so addicted to wanting to have a life without Antonio, but I never imagined my life without him.

I thought that I could go out and do as I pleased with Donte and Antonio would always be there waiting for me. I thought that whatever I did, Antonio would always forgive me. He would always be there because he has always been there.

I know that I talked big shit about how I would leave Antonio for Donte and maybe if things were as I thought they would be, with Antonio sitting at home waiting for me to come home to him, that would still ring true. And even though I was still in love with them both, Donte had proven to be fickle. I have no clue what changed between us, but he was definitely showing me a different version of himself. A version I didn't like too much. I had invested so much into this man, upgrading his life in ways no one would have thought. I didn't know if I could completely let him go. Sitting here watching my husband fawn over this woman, I knew that I would never be able to let him go either. He was mine. So, Emily would have to back the fuck off.

I downed the rest of my drink, completely over the sight before me. I didn't need to see anymore. I needed to go home and re-collect myself. I had to figure out what I was going to do to make sure that my husband stayed my husband

and out of Emily's grasp and that Donte stayed mine also. I snatched my purse from the bar top and walked out of the restaurant and headed to my car. The drive home was a blur. The only thing that I remember is pulling into my driveway and ambling up the walkway to my front door. My heart was crying out for my husband, but my body was calling out for Donte.

Now I knew the true meaning of wanting your cake and eating it too. This addiction to this man was ruining my marriage. But I still wasn't strong enough to cure myself from the urge to want to be with him. I was confused as fuck. I didn't know what I wanted. I do know that I didn't want to choose, and if things went my way, then I wouldn't have to.

Eric Sawyer

Me telling Jazelle about Emily and Antonio was supposed to do one thing and one thing only. It was supposed to push her more into Donte's arms and further away from Antonio. I debated on rather I wanted to tell her the truth about Antonio and I or lie and tell her that Emily and Antonio were together.

The lie seemed more believable. No woman would believe that her husband was a downlow gay man. I was supposed to meet them both, Antonio and Emily, tonight for dinner, but I cancelled so that when Jazelle showed up, she would only see them two together. I did, however, make sure that I was at the restaurant to observe the way Jazelle reacted to seeing Antonio sit with that beautiful woman all night. I watched her watch them, and she looked like she wanted to cry sitting on that barstool staring at Antonio and Emily.

I did feel bad for her. My intentions weren't to hurt Jazelle. Like I said before, she was a nice person and everything that I thought a woman should be. But she was one of the few things that was blocking me from taking my rightful spot in Antonio's life. Plus, she was cheating on him, so she couldn't have been that much in love with him. It was obvious to me that Donte was where she wanted to be. I was just helping her along in the process.

So, while I was waiting for Antonio to grieve his wife

leaving him, and me being his shoulder to cry on, I needed to figure out what I was going to do about my father. Now that the odds were in my favor for Antonio to be mine, I only had my father standing in my way. He was my biggest obstacle. He would never allow me to be with the man of my dreams. According to him, I was an abomination and a disgrace to him, the church and God. So, I knew that I had to get rid of him, but the question was how. How was I going to get rid of him without any of the blame being put on me? I wasn't trying to go to jail on a murder charge. Anything that I did would have to be ruled accidental or a suicide.

It had to be something that no one saw coming, and I had to make sure that I was still acting completely normal towards him. I wasn't just this evil guy who just went around killing old ass preachers or parents or no shit like that. I would say that I was just a fed-up man that was ready to move forward with my life and willing to do so at any cost.

For the past few weeks, I've been using the computers at the local library to do research on undetectable poisons. I couldn't risk using my own computer and risk the cops tracing my searches back to my IP Address. I watched a lot of ID channel and Snapped, so I knew a little bit on avoiding certain shit so I wouldn't get caught.

Offing my father would do more than just free me to be with Antonio, it would free me from the beatings that he was still putting on me. Free me from the shame that he always made me feel. It would free Sharise from me. I hated having to string her along, and she deserved so much better than to be with a man that was not attracted to her sexually and that could never love her in the way that she needed to be loved. It would also free my mother from his controlling and vindictive ways. Though she would never say it out loud, I knew that she was tired of getting her ass beat also. That's why it absolutely had to be done. There were no ifs, and's, buts or maybes. Even unknowingly, there were people who were counting on me to complete this task. It had to be sooner than later.

Three Weeks Later

Today my father was coming over for his usual breakfast and bash on Eric parade as he did every damn day. I was nervous and antsy about the events that would be taking place today. I felt horrible for what I was about to do, but it had to be done. I paced my living room numerous times before I decided to turn on some music to calm my nerve. I turned on my tv and put it on the pandora app. I turned on some Nipsy Hussle 'Victory Lap' and took a seat on my couch and waited for my father to make his arrival.

I already had the table set with the breakfast that I prepared a short time earlier. He hated to show up and there was no food, or his plate wasn't already made. So, to prevent him from going in on me as soon as he walked through the door, I made sure that I handled that. It was crazy because even knowing what I was about to do, I was still seeking his acceptance, still wanting to make him happy. The hold that he had on me was incredible. I walked back over to the dining room table to make sure everything looked up to par. I was so fucking antsy right now.

It was a beautiful breakfast consisting of Belgian Waffles, thick cut maple bacon, grapes, strawberries, fluffy scrambled eggs, spicy Jimmy Dean sausage, and buttery grits. I thought that I would make it nice for him seeing that hopefully if everything went according to plan, it would be his last meal.

Finally, I heard my doorbell ring and rapid knocking afterwards. His impatience was one thing that I was not going to miss. I rushed to open the door to let him in. He pushed past me and entered my home as if he paid the mortgage here.

"Took you long enough to answer the damned door son." He said making sure to put emphasis and a touch of sarcasm on the word 'son.'

"I was getting the table ready dad. I came to the door as soon as I heard the doorbell ring," I said smacking my lips.

SMACK SMACK

He slapped the shit out of me twice across my face. I was fucking livid. I was absolutely tired of this shit.

"You'll get enough of talking out of turn Eric. I should have named you Erica since you think that you're a woman. Smacking your lips and carrying on. Speak to me like that again, and it will be much worse," my father gritted.

"I didn't mean to disrespect you dad," I said feeling like the scared little boy that I was whenever I was around my father.

"Why do you treat me this way? Why is it so hard for you to accept me for who, and what I am. You're a preacher for God's sake. You are supposed to try to follow in the footsteps of our father and practice forgiveness and compassion. You have neither of those," I said.

My voice was shaky, but it was something that I never had the nerve to ask him before. I had to have some questions answered before he was no longer here to terrorize our family with his bullshit.

"I will never have either of those things when it comes to you. You disgust me in the worst way. I have no clue where your mother, and I went wrong with you. You chose to TRY to live a life that you knew I would never accept. You weren't raised to like or toy around with men. It's a devil inside of you, and I have been trying to beat it out of you ever since it surfaced."

"I understand dad. I will be better. I will be the son that you've always wanted," I lied.

I was who I was, and that would never change. I had to put on this front to get his old ass where I wanted him.

"Come take a seat at the table, I have your plate already made. What would you like to drink?'' I asked ready to get this shit over with.

I was wasting my time and breath on my dad. He would never change. He would always be this evil man hiding behind his bible and a pulpit. I hoped that he had life insurance so that I could ensure that my mother would be well taken care of. But even if it was left up to me to take care of her, this would be worth that little sacrifice.

"Bring me a glass of Orange Juice," he demanded already digging into his plate of food. I turned around on my heels and headed to the kitchen to prepare his last drink. Since my dining room was closed off from my kitchen, it allowed me ample opportunity to do what I needed to do. I reached into my cabinet to get a tall glass for his juice and sat it on the counter. I looked over my shoulder to make sure that I was still in the clear as I pulled the small glass bottle from my kitchen drawer. I was shaking like a hoe in the Health Department. My hands were so sweaty that I was afraid that I would drop the fucking bottle on the ground.

While doing my research online, I came across a

website that gave me all of the information I needed. I wanted something that would kill him quickly but was virtually undetectable to the doctor that does the autopsy. They said that the best poison to use was one that breaks down into elements that are natural in the body. After doing more research, I found a website that sold Aconite poisoning. It came in the form of a beautiful purple flower that was broken down into tiny pieces. Every part of that flower was laced with the toxin Aconitine. Just touching this plant could cause tingles, numbness and heart problems which is why it was packaged in this glass so that I couldn't touch it. The symptoms were even worse when ingested. This toxin was water soluble and had no flavor which is why I found myself emptying over half of the jar into my father's orange juice. I chose to put it in his drink so that I wouldn't fuck up somehow and mix our plates up then kill my own damn self. After I poured the poison into his glass, I took a spoon and carefully mixed it to make sure that all of the flowers were properly dissolved so that he wouldn't suspect anything.

First, he would begin to sweat and vomit. Then he would have intense pain in every part of his body. He would then experience paralysis of his skeletal muscles. Lastly, he would have life-threatening arrhythmias back to back that mimics a massive heart attack. Then he would die, and I would have my life back.

I walked back into the dining room and placed his drink in front of him and sat at the other end of the table. He didn't even acknowledge me or the damn drink I placed before him. He just continued eating his food. I was starting to feel a little uneasy, but there was no backing out. The show had to go on.

"So how is my future daughter-in-law Sharise? I haven't seen her around here the past few months. Did she find out you were funny or something?" He laughed.

He was sitting in my house, eating my food, and laughing at my expense. This man was truly a piece of work.

"We are not together anymore. She needed some space, and so did I," I replied keeping it as vague as I could.

"Figures someone like you, wouldn't be able to keep a fine piece of woman like that." He said picking up his glass and putting it to his lips.

"I should have kept her for myself." He whispered into the glass like I wouldn't be able to hear his old ass.

My anxiety was on ten right now. I was clinching my ass cheeks together so tight that if I had a lump of coal in my ass, I would shit out a diamond.

I watched him as he downed the entire glass of juice. He scrunched his face up and slammed the glass down on to the table like the shit was good to him. Figures that the nigga would like the taste of poison with his evil ass.

"Go get me another glass of juice," he demanded.

I rose from my seat and walked over to him to grab the glass from the table. I made my way into the kitchen to pour him another glass of juice. I contemplated pouring the remainder of the Aconite poisoning into his glass, but for some reason, I decided against it. I walked back to the dining room to hand my father his drink. When I looked into his face, he was sweating profusely. It was coming down his face like he had just ran a fucking marathon.

"Turn the fucking air on. Why is it so damned hot in here?" He said struggling to breathe. I smirked at him knowing that this would be the last time he talked shit to me.

Suddenly his face dropped, void of all emotion, and his arms went limp and dropped to his sides. His head flew back, and he began to gurgle vomit. I rushed over to him, and I pushed him out the chair on to the ground. I wanted to make sure that he didn't not get a bunch of vomit on my fucking table or on his clothes.

I watched him as he lay on the floor shaking and convulsing looking weak and helpless. The same way that I have been for most of my life. He looked up at me with so much fear in his eyes. Like he knew what I had done to him. Even though he could not speak, I knew that he was cursing me to hell. Now I knew how he must have felt all these years. I felt so in control of my life, and powerful in this moment.

The roles were reversed, and I watched my father's body go completely limp from the paralysis. His eyes were still open and staring into my soul. I reached down to put my hand on his chest to see if it was still beating. It was a very faint heartbeat, but he was still alive. I looked him in his eyes so that I could get a few things off of my chest.

"How does it feel now?" I said menacingly.

"How does it feel to be at my mercy? How does it feel to know that you're going to die at the hands of the person that you hate the most, the person that disgusts you in the worst way? HAHAHAHAHA Looks like I won Dad. I might even take over your church and be the first openly gay pastor in Ft. Worth." I wasn't doing that shit, but it was funny to watch his eyes bulge out of his head. Even while he was dying, he was still worried about what his precious church congregation thought of him. Sad.

His eyes started to roll to the back of his head until I only saw the whites of his eyeballs. He stopped breathing, and I could see the life leave his body. It was done. I did it. He was gone, and I was happy. I deserved a better father than the one that God gave me. He wasn't good enough for me or my mother.

I went back into the kitchen and began to make a bucket of water with dawn dish soap to clean the vomit from my father and my floor. I made sure not to use bleach because bleach and a dead person always made cops suspicious. I walked back into the dining room and bent down on the ground next to my father and began to wipe up his vomit. His eyes were still wide open. They held a look in them that I couldn't describe. Shock. Fear. Regret. I don't know. I stared at him a little longer, then I used my fingers to shut his eyes for good.

I cleaned him up and all of the dishes from the breakfast that we ate. Once I got rid of all the cleaning supplies and there was just my dad's dead body lying in the middle of my dining room floor. I grabbed my phone from my pocket and headed towards the living room. I knew that I had to call 911 to report that my father had a 'heart attack' but I needed for my grief to sound believable.

I sat there and thought of all the things that made me sad. I thought of all the ways that my father and mother had hurt me over the years. I thought of all the vulgar names I had been called and all the times that he had beaten my ass. All of these things brought up emotions in me that were most times hard to deal with. As soon as I felt the emotions break through my veil, I called the 911 operator and explained to her that my father had just had a heart attack and that he was unresponsive. She told me that an ambulance was on its way and to try and start CPR. I lied to her and told that I was when really, I was just sitting here staring at him.

I heard the ambulance in the near distance, and I went and opened the front door so that they could just rush right in and prepared myself for the questions that were to come. Finally, the EMTs rushed into my home and started putting tubes down his throat and an oxygen mask on his face.

After about 20 minutes of trying to resuscitate my father, the EMTS pronounced him dead at 10:45 am. They placed him on a gurney and rolled him out of my house and out of my life covered in a white sheet.

When I was finally alone, I cried, hard. I cried for my mother. I cried for myself. I cried for everyone who had been hurt by my father. I cried because finally, I was free.

Donte Abraham

It's crazy how shit happens. How meeting Antonio led me to meeting Jazelle, which in turn led me to have the pleasure of meeting Karli. We have spent a lot of time together these past few weeks. I already liked her from the beginning, but that feeling was even more intense now. She was finally starting to soften up, and let me in. I was starting to see something in her that I didn't know was there. There was a lot more to her than the overzealous person that you all were getting to know. All Karli needed was for someone to love her right. Someone to show her that life is more than just playing with people's emotions and lives.

I wanted to give her everything that she wanted because no one had ever done that for her before, and I wanted to show her something different. But even more than that, I wanted to finish my business with Jazelle. Karli had been occupying most of my time so I haven't been spending as much time with Jazelle. I could tell that it was starting to have an effect on her and our relationship, so I needed to get back in her good graces until she came through on that job. I just had to figure out how.

Right now, I was headed to the gym to meet up with Antonio and Eric to get a work out in. We hadn't met up in a while seeing that I was splitting all of my time between

HE WASN'T GOOD ENOUGH FOR ME

Antonio's wife and her best friend. I kind of wanted to see where his head was. I wanted to see if things were bad with them or if he didn't even notice the difference in his wife. Because she was indeed different. The way she walked was different. The way she talked was different. The way she wore her hair and the way she dressed was different. I'm sure that if I could see the change in her, then Antonio could also see it. She was coming out of her shell and that was all thanks to me.

A couple of weeks after Karli and I hooked up, I finally made time for Jazelle. I'm not so sure that I'm glad that I did. I finally gave in and gave her some dick; she's been super clingy and possessive ever since. But that was nothing that I couldn't deal with.

As I pulled in to the parking lot of Planet Fitness, I noticed Antonio and Eric in front of the building having what seemed to be a heated argument. I mean we all work out together, but as far as I know, they didn't know each other well enough to be having an argument about anything. Whatever they were arguing about had to be intense because Mya and I had been having these types of arguments, with the flying hands and the straining veins lately. So, I knew a real spat if I didn't know anything else. I sat in my car and watched them go back and forth with each other until I got bored and decided to get out of my car and see what this was all about. As soon as they seen me walking up to them, the argument stopped, and Antonio walked off into the gym without saying another word to either of us.

"Yo, what was that about?" I asked Eric.

"It looks like ya'll was having a lover's spat," I laughed jokingly.

"What!? Man come on. Don't disrespect me like that! That nigga was tripping out over his wife and was venting to me about it. That's what that was," Eric replied.

"What about his wife. Do that nigga know she getting those cheeks beat by someone else or what? You didn't say anything did you?"

"Nah I didn't say anything. You know me better than that. But it sounds like you scared for Antonio to find out. I know you ain't scared," Eric smirked.

I wanted to slap the shit out of him. Donte wasn't scared of no muthafucking body. I've never been, and I never will be. You know what? I take that back. I was scared of Mya's crazy ass. My wife was not all the way there in the head.

"Man, naw I ain't scared of no damn Antonio. I just don't feel like fighting over a woman that I don't really want."

"What the hell you mean you don't want Jazelle? You been MIA for the last few weeks all up in her space. How can you not want her?" Eric asked a little too concerned about my whereabouts and my fucking business.

"Actually, since you all up in my damn business, I've been all up in Karli's space. I've been kicking it with her real tough, and I like her. You know she's more my type anyway. But there is more to her than just the surface. She got layers bro, and I've been peeling all of them back," I bragged.

"Nigga I'm disgusted. Karli is trash. She ain't no better than Mya. You going backwards my dude," he replied agitated.

"What does it matter to you who I'm fucking? You are doing a lot right now Eric. Chill out and let's go in there with Antonio and get this workout in," I said walking off

On some real shit, I couldn't be worried about what Eric thought about what I was doing. I know that he was probably just being a good friend and didn't want me to make the same mistake with Karli that I made with Mya. Honestly, although Karli was ratchet like Mya, she was different. She was more than what met the eye. She had a lot of depth to her, and I could see myself being with her in the future.

Unlike Jazelle, Karli had a backbone, and wouldn't allow me to walk all over her. That's the kind of woman that I needed. Strong. Assertive. Bold. Not docile, and submissive, too kind and nice. That just didn't do it for me.

So, Eric could kiss my ass with his opinions on what I was doing with Karli. Jazelle was just a means to an end for me, and even though it was fun, and she had some good pussy, once she got me this job as Head Chef at her friends' restaurant, I was out.

Then Antonio can quit crying over his wife.

I would have what I wanted from him from the beginning. I would have a life that Jazelle handed me on a silver platter. A life that really didn't take too much effort out of me. Letting her down easy would be the hard part. She was invested in me, hell, she even talked about leaving her husband. I didn't want her to do that. I wanted them to work shit out so I could make my exit peacefully. But I don't think that Jazelle was going to make it that easy for me. I knew that she loved me. But it was the risk that I was willing to take in order to have all of the things that I felt like I deserved.

Once Eric and I made it inside and met Antonio at the weight lifting area of the gym, we worked out in pure silence. I had my earphones on listening to some Meek Mills, thinking about what my next move would be. At this point, I didn't know which way to go because I had never played with people's marriage and lives and shit before. I was no better than Mya trapping me in a marriage and into parenthood with a child that she knew didn't belong to me or Karli purposely sleeping with other women's husbands.

Speaking of Mya, she had been acting different lately. At one point it seemed as if she was trying to make things work in our marriage. But as of a couple of weeks ago, around the same time that I started fucking on Karli, she's been fighting and arguing with me anytime we were around each other. Not like the fighting we were doing before when she was just tired of me. It was different like I had hurt her in some way. Whatever it was, I would be glad when I no longer had to deal with her at all.

After I was done lifting weights, I went to get on the treadmill. These muthafuckas, Antonio and Eric, were spotting each other and working out together and just leaving me out. I felt like the little nigga that got picked last to be on the team at recess. I wasn't tripping though.

I was thinking about asking Antonio to meet me for dinner and to bring his wife. But I didn't know how to present it to him without sounding all suspect and shit. I wanted to see how Jazelle would handle seeing Antonio, and I in the same room. It would be my first step in strategically backing off just a little bit. After I secured the job, then I could back out all the way. I did 30 minutes on the treadmill and hopped off to go talk to Antonio. He was sitting on a weight bench downing some water when I approached him.

"What's up Antonio? We haven't worked out together in a while. What's been up dude?" I asked trying to start a conversation.

"Man, nothing much, just chilling, working, and trying to keep my little bourgeois wife happy."

"Lying ass," I thought.

"Alright man, that sounds good. There ain't nothing better than making the old lady happy," I said indulging him in his lie. I already knew that he wasn't keeping her happy, she always told me everything that went on between them.

"Exactly. I was thinking about taking her out soon. You should join us for dinner. It'll be sometime this week," he said

"Yea, we can do that. Text me the time and place. Do I need to bring a date?" I asked, happy as hell that he brought up meeting up with him and Jazelle first.

"Yea but if you don't have one, I can just have Jazelle bring her friend."

"Cool. Let's do that. I don't feel like looking through my little black book," I joked.

"I'll text you details later," Antonio stated while getting up to leave. He dapped me up and turned to exit the building.

I was excited about dinner. I knew that Jazelle was going to trip the fuck out when she saw me sitting there. She didn't even know that I knew Antonio at all. I never told her because I felt like she would be afraid to move forward with me and do the things that I needed her to do. I knew that this was going to make her feel a way about me. I also knew that the friend that he was going to tell her to invite was going to be Karli. That was the only homegirl that she had a tight personal relationship with that I knew of. I was hoping that I could keep what Karli and I had going on at bay. That shit was going to be hard because I had developed strong feelings for her in a short period of time.

I was still sitting at the weight benches when Eric came back from the bathroom.

"Where did Tony go?" He asked me.

"Nigga who the fuck is Tony?" I asked him looking at him sideways.

"Antonio!" He said smacking his lips at me. I hated when he did that shit.

"He's gone, but he wants us to have dinner with him this week. You down to roll with me?" I asked him purposely leaving out the fact that Jazelle and Karli would be there. I knew that he didn't like Karli and would probably say no to going. I didn't want him lecturing and preaching to me about being around Jazelle while her husband was there. This shit was going to be one for the books.

"Yea my schedule should be clear so I'll be able to roll through,'' he said excitedly.

"Aight bet. I'll send you the details once he sends

them to me. I'm out though. I got to slide by the house really quick and deal with Mya," I replied while walking towards the exit.

I got in my car and headed towards me and Mya's home. I knew that it was going to be some shit when I got there. She had been texting me all day, and I had been ignoring her. She was tripping on me telling me that she wanted me to adopt her son and shit. She knew that once I got this job I was leaving, and I guess that was her way of trying to keep me in her life.

That shit wasn't happening. I hate to sound fucked up, but once I left her, I was leaving her kid too. I treated him like he was mine, but the fact remains that he's not. There is nothing that Mya could do that would make me stay with her or even deal with her after I made my exit. That ship had sailed, and it was all her fault. This whole time that I've been messing around with Jazelle and Karli made me want to get away from Mya even more. There was so much more life out there, and this bitch had been wasting mine for years.

Once I pulled up in the driveway and walked to the door, she swung the door open before I could even put my key into the lock. Bitch must have been looking out of the window for me.

"About time you brought my car back Donte." She stomped away from the door.

I didn't even respond to her. I just walked through the living room and into the kitchen to get me something cold to drink. She stood in the entryway of the kitchen with her arms crossed while staring me down, I'm guessing waiting on me to reply.

"I don't know what you want me to say, Mya, I'm here now so if you got somewhere to be, then go ahead and go," I said already getting agitated. I haven't been here five minutes yet, and she was already working on my damn nerves.

"That's not the point Donte!! I know that you're cheating on me. You couldn't be more obvious about it. You don't even try with me like you used to. For the past few months I've been trying to fix things with you, and you don't even look at a bitch twice. I been throwing pussy at you left and right and you acting like you can't stand the sight of me. At least before you would fuck me for room and board, now you don't even give a fuck about that. So, what's up? What's your deal? She ranted.

"Maaaan, Mya, you already know that I haven't fucked with you since you put that baby on me. I've been making changes in my life, trying to do the things I've always wanted to do, things that you wouldn't support me in. Now all of a sudden you want to work things out with me. I told you I wanted to be a chef. I asked you to help me, but you laughed at me like I was telling a fucking joke. I asked you to help me get into culinary school, but you turned your nose up at me. You've always looked down on me because I wasn't moving at the pace that you thought I should. So yea! I got a woman that would help me with all of that.

She helped me get into school, she helped me get my credit straight, and she's helping me secure a job as head chef at the restaurant in Reunion Tower. All of the things that you, my WIFE, should have done. You should have been down for me when I was down. Now that you see me coming up, you want to 'work things out.'. Why not try to work it out before you cheated on me. and brought home a baby that wasn't mine? I had to watch your baby and fuck on you for you to even want to give me a place to live. I can't respect you for that man. I can't forgive you," I said.

I was finally able to get all of this off of my chest without her throwing shit and cursing me out. I hoped that she was listening and coming to terms with the fact that she fucked us up and she couldn't fix us.

"I get it, Donte. I fucked us up. I know that. But she can't have you. You are my husband. Does this bitch even know that you have a wife? Does she know that you aren't available to her? I will not share you with her, and I will not let her take you from me. Anything can be repaired if you really want it. I understand that I all but handed you over to

HE WASN'T GOOD ENOUGH FOR ME

her. But that all stops here. If I can't have you, then she most definitely will not," she replied with tears in her eyes.

To my surprise, Karli wasn't too happy about my wife. She had even told me that I could move in with her so that I would leave Mya sooner. But I wanted to move out into my own shit. I will never put myself in the same situation that I'm currently in with Mya.

If I didn't know any better, I would have thought that Mya was being sincere. But I knew Mya, and I knew that this was just a competition to her. She didn't want me, but she didn't want to lose me to someone else. I couldn't be bothered with her fickle ass. It was already written.

Karli Washington

"Alright! Damn! I said that I'll be by there today!! Stop fucking calling me!" I yelled into the phone. Robert had been calling me nonstop the last few months trying to get me to come and see my sick mother. I hadn't made the time yet because I been busy as fuck. But I know that I needed to do my part as a daughter and at least show my face.

"Okay baby girl! I just wanted to make sure that you were going to come. She's been asking about you almost every day. But I'll let her know that you will be here today. I'm sorry for calling so much," Robert replied. Sounding pitiful as fuck.

"Alright BYEEEEE!!!" I sang into the phone and hung up on his ass. Fuck him!

Ever since I became an adult, he had been trying to apologize to me for choosing my mother over me. I wasn't pressed though. I didn't need any apology from his old ass. I did need one from my mother though. I wanted her to apologize for not protecting me against her Chester Molester ass husband. But I knew that she would never offer me an apology. And rather I wanted to or not, I would have to be ok with that. It was exhausting being angry all the time. I didn't want to be this way anymore. I wanted to be loved. I wanted to be happy. And even though Donte was trying to give me that, he couldn't, because he wasn't mine. He still belonged to someone else.

"Damn baby! Why you have to be so mean to the old man?" Donte asked from his place on my lap.

I had never told Donte about what happened to me when I was a child. So, he didn't know why I hated Robert and my mother so much. I wanted to tell him, but I didn't want to be judged about something that happened so long ago. But maybe it would give him a better understanding of me and why I was the way that I was. Against my better judgment, I told him only what I felt like he needed to know.

"Because baby! When I was 15 years old, the nigga raped me. He raped me every night while my mother was at work. He did it so much that after a while I began to think the shit was normal so I stopped fighting it. I let him do whatever he wanted to me and went along with whatever he said. He told me that I was his girlfriend, so I believed him. He told me that he loved me and that he would leave my mother and be with me, so I believed him. But he was just manipulating my young mind. I told my bad built ass mama about it, and she told me that I was lying and that no man would choose a child over a real woman. So, fuck her and fuck him," I ranted.

"I'm so sorry that happened to you, Karli. I wish that I could have protected you from that nigga. But I guarantee you that nobody will put their hands on yo fine ass ever again....... unless it's me," he said.

"Nigga how was you gone protect me if you ain't even know me?" I laughed.

"HAHAHA, you know what the hell I meant Karli with yo goofy ass."

"Yea! Yea! Yea, but on a more serious note, when are you going to end this shit with Jazelle? There are too many women in your life, and I'm feeling last place like a muthafucka, and I'm not liking this shit AT ALL!'' I asked him.

"Baby I already told you that I'm waiting on this job to come through, and then I'm done with her. You are not last place baby. You are definitely number one in my book. You already know what it is girl."

"You ain't fucking her is you Donte? If you are then you need to tell me the truth. I dropped everybody for you but you still have both Jazelle and your wife." I whined to him

"I'm not having sex with either one of them Karli. You are just letting your insecurities take over right now. I'm leaving my wife and I'm only using Jazelle. I want you though. Only you." He reassured me.

Yea Donte finally broke down a couple of weeks ago after I wouldn't stop hounding him about Jazelle. He told me about his little stupid ass plan to lead Jazelle on so that she could help him with the things that I guess he felt he couldn't do on his own. I thought that there was a better way to go about it, but I guess that means nothing coming from me. I thrived on destroying relationships and shit. But Jazelle had been my friend for years, and I know how she feels about Donte. Even knowing that, I couldn't let her have him. I was falling in love with him. We had been sneaking around for a few months now, and I was ready for him to drop these other women so that I could be his number one.

I was kind of afraid of being with him exclusively because I knew that with all the dirt that I've done in my life, someone or something was going to come and snatch my happiness from me and I wasn't going to know how to deal with it. If I let myself fall completely for Donte like my heart wanted me to, something was bound to happen. Either some funky ass bitch was gone fuck on my man, or I was gone go back to my old ways and fuck on somebody else's husband. I needed to be able to protect us. Karma was a bitch that I didn't want to meet. She was rude and ugly and had no fucking couth.

"Ok and what about your wife? When are you going to handle that situation? I already told yo ass that you could come and live with me if your sole purpose of being there was so that you would have a place to stay. Unless that's not the real reason for you being there."

"Look, baby. I know that you extended the invitation for me to come and live with you. But you have to understand where I'm coming from. I never want to be put in the same situation that I'm in now with Mya. I don't want a woman to ever be able to have so much control over me. I don't want you to be able to put me out when you're mad at me."

"I would never do that to you though Donte," I rebutted.

"You may not, but you would have the power to. When we move in together, it will be both of our home. It will be something that we acquired together. I want you, but I want you the right way. You are enough for me."

A bitch heart fucking melted. I ain't never heard no shit like this before. Not being directed at me. I had to hold back my tears cause a real bitch like me didn't cry, but I sure did want to. I couldn't believe that this could happen to cold-hearted Karli. But it was, and I was loving it.

"I can accept that," I said as I leaned down to kiss his soft lips.

Sex with Donte was everything I never knew that I wanted. He took care of my body and always put my needs before his own. I never had to chase a nut because he always wrapped it in a bow and handed it to me. Like a real man.

That soft peck I placed on his lips turned into a deep intoxicating kiss that took all of the breath out of my lungs. He lifted up out of my lap and sat on the couch next to me. He picked me up and placed me in his lap so that I was straddling him. Even though I had places to be today, nothing was better than the place that Donte was about to take me to.

He started kissing and licking on my neck. He knew that was my spot. I threw my head back to give him more access. He pulled my tube top down and exposed both of my breast. My nipples were harder than diamond and aching for the warmth of his mouth. He sucked my right breast into his mouth while he rolled my left one between his index finger and his thumb. The feeling sent chills down my spine.

My pussy leaked from the attention he was showing my body, and I'm sure that he could feel the warmth of my middle through the thin basketball shorts that he had on. My body took over as I gyrated my pussy over his hard dick. I wanted him to penetrate my body like he had already penetrated my mind and my heart. I reached up under myself to pull his dick from his shorts. I lifted up so that he could pull my tiny shorts to the side. My pussy was wet, but that still didn't allow easy entry. Donte's dick was big as fuck, and my pussy was still learning how to handle him.

Once all of him was inside of me, I perched myself up on my feet and moved my body up and down his dick so slow trying to adjust to him. He grabbed two hand fulls of both of my ass cheeks and guided me up and down in a way that allowed him to hit that gushy spot in the back of my pussy at just the right tempo. I was leaking pussy juice all over his lap.

"Donte baby please don't stop. I'm about to cuuuuuuuuuummm," I moaned with my head thrown back and my mouth wide open. I had tears rolling down my face from the pleasure that he was giving me. I wanted to have this feeling forever.

After Donte and I went a couple of more rounds, I was exhausted. He had worn me out, but I still had to make my way over to my mothers. I've been dreading this moment for months.

"Baby as much as I would love to lay up under you for the rest of the day, I got to head out to go see about my ugl'ass mama. So, I'm about to go shower and get ready to head out."

"Ok I'ma shower with you," Donte said.

"Uh uh, nigga. No! If you get in the shower with me, I will never get over to my mama's. Nope. You tried it though," I laughed and sauntered towards my bathroom.

I wish that I didn't have to leave him, but it was better to go ahead and get this shit over with. I could speak my peace and be done with both Robert and my mother, Dara's country ass.

Once I washed the sex from my body, I got out and dried off so that I could get dressed. I didn't need to do too much to myself because I was already fine as hell. And since being with Donte, I didn't feel the need to cake makeup on my face as if I was trying to hide the person that I really was. I sat at my vanity and just put on my eyebrows cause on some real shit, a bitch eyebrows was sparse as fuck, and I threw on some Fenty Gloss Bomb Lip Luminizer.

I went to my closet and threw on some black ripped knee canopy pants from Fashion Nova that I saw Jazelle order before and a white boyfriend shirt I got from the sales rack at Macy's. I decided to put on some white and black Adidas just in case I had to beat Robert or my mama's ass. I didn't want to be balancing on no heels. I wanted to be flat on my feet and ready to whoop some ass if need be. I grabbed my purse off of my dresser headed to the living room where I heard Donte watching ESPN.

"I'm heading out baby. I should be back within the next couple of hours. Maybe before that since I can foresee my mama cussing my ass out, and me dipping out of that bitch within twenty minutes of me getting there," I said to him

"You sure you don't want me to go with you. You know, in case that nigga Robert try to jump stupid, and I have to beat his ass." Donte said making me laugh because I was just literally thinking the same thing.

"You know what? Maybe we do belong together because I literally just thought the same thing. That's why I put tennis shoes on in case I had to get down up in that bitch. But naw baby I'll be good. If I need you, I will definitely call you. I'll text you the address right now just in case. Are you gone be here when I get back or are you leaving?"

"I don't have plans right now so I should be here, but if anything comes up I'll let you know."

"Alright baby. See you later," I said while blowing a kiss to my future.

I walked out of my apartment building and to my car. I put the address to my egg donors house in my car GPS and headed to the south side where my mama lived. I couldn't remember how to get there exactly which is why I had the GPS on, but I knew she lived in a raggedy ass house on Hattie St and it was right in the middle of the fucking hood.

As I was riding silently in my car trying to get my mind right, I got a call on my cell phone. I thought it was Robert bothering the fuck out of me again, but it was that bugga boo ass nigga Javier. I was so ready to get rid of his ass. I haven't checked in on Antonio in a while, but I was hoping that he listened to me and stop fucking with Emily. Obviously, he hasn't because Javier was still calling my fucking phone. I decided to entertain him at least until I made it to my destination.

"Hell fucking lo nigga!! Why the fuck you still calling me???? This is what I get for throwing this good ass pussy on you, now yo ass don't know how or when to let the fuck go."

"Damn girl don't do me like that. Why you switching up on me all of a sudden?"

"All of a sudden?! Nigga I been trying to get rid of you for months now. Where is yo fucking wife? Go make shit work with her and leave me the hell alone! I got a man now anyway, and he would not be happy about you calling me the way that you have been. You act like you can't catch a hint." I yelled at him. I was starting to think that he was one of those niggas that liked when a bitch cussed his ass the fuck out. This man was stressing me the hell out.

"A man!!" He exclaimed.

"We both know you ain't built for one man Karli. You ain't the type of woman that a man settles down with. You a fun girl. That's it, and that's all. Talking about you got a man. We'll see how long that shit last," he laughed.

"Yet here you are on my line begging me to fuck with you. I'm tired of yo creepy ass. BYE BITCH!!." I yelled and hung up the phone.

My feelings were actually kind of hurt. I was

evolving, and this nigga was still trying to keep me in a box that I was fighting hard to get out of.

Everybody wanted me to be the same Bitch that I had always been. Nobody wanted me to grow. Donte made me want to better. For the first time, I actually felt like I could be better.

I deserved to be loved just like Jazelle did. Hell, just like anybody else did.

After driving a few more minutes, I pulled up in front of Dara's house. There were little bad ass kids playing basketball in the street cursing each other out. This raggedy ass house didn't even have a fucking driveway. I pulled up alongside the curb and prayed that nobody hit my shit and that none of these bad ass kids hit my car with they're basketballs. I got out of my car and walked towards the house. There were bars on the window and the screen door, so you know shit went down in this neighborhood. I'm not throwing shade at the hood because I grew up in the hood. But I didn't live here anymore, and I didn't hang around in the hood. You can say I forgot where I came from all you want, but I don't give any fucks. I didn't fuck around out here. I knocked on the gated screen door two or three times before Robert brought his old beat up baby looking ass to the door and answered it.

"Hey, baby girl. I'm so happy that you were able to

stop by and see us," he said while reaching out for a hug.

"Ewww stop calling me that, and don't try to touch me at all with yo nasty ass old ass gremlin fingers," I said sidestepping his ass.

It was no love over here so he could stop with all of the fucking antics. He knew exactly what he had done to me, but I guess he expected me to believe he had fucking amnesia now.

"Where is Dara?" I asked him.

"Your mother is in the back room. Gone on and head on back there. She'll be happy to see you." He said and sat his fat ass on the couch.

He didn't use to be fat…… He used to be fine and cut up. But time had caught up to him, and so had gravity. He was sagging in places I didn't know could sag. This nigga earlobes were sagging, like what the fuck, he grossed me out.

I walked to the back of the house into a room that was set up like a hospital. I guess the bitch really was sick. That bitch Karma had already knocked on Dara's door, or the bitch probably just broke up in this bitch since we were in the heart of the hood.

I stood at the door and looked at her. She looked nothing like the woman that I remembered. I look just like my mother did when she was younger. She was beautiful. But now she looked aged and tired and well, just sick.

"There you go you, raggedy bitch! I been waiting on you for months. You hate me that much that it took you this long to come by and check on me? She croaked.

She sounded like she smoked 5 packs of cigarettes a damn day with that hard, coarse, crunchy ass voice. I bet her damn breath stank.

"Yea it took me this long because I didn't want to hear you talk shit like you doing now. What the hell is wrong with you anyway? Before I come closer into this room, is the shit contagious?" I asked serious as hell.

I wasn't trying to catch nothing from this mean ass woman. She done already gave me enough bullshit.

"I got the cancers." she said. I tried my hardest not to laugh. What the fuck was the cancers? This woman was country as hell.

"What kind of cancer do you have Dara? And why did you want me to come see you so bad?" I asked her.

"I got the lung and the throat cancers. I wanted you to come see me so that you can see what you done did to me." This bitch said with a straight face.

"What the hell you mean what I did to you? I didn't do shit to your hateful ass. You the one that started smoking them cigarettes. I ain't have shit to do with that."

"Well. If you wasn't fucking my husband, I wouldn't have been stressed enough to start smoking. It all leads back to you. You are a whore, and you got the bad juju on you. You are bad luck. Get thee out of her Satan," She had the nerve to say.

"You mean if your husband wasn't fucking on me. I was fifteen years old. I wasn't old enough to consent to anything that your man did to me. If you gonna be mad at anybody, you should be mad at that ugly ass nigga in there and be mad at yourself. I'm leaving. I don't give a fuck if you roll over and die right now. I thought coming to see you would help me with dealing with the situation that happened with Robert. But you're just as much part of the problem as he is. Both of y'all ain't shit," I yelled.

"Hey hey now. What the hell is going on up in here." Robert walked into the room and asked.

"Shut yo ass up you round, rotund mothafucka!!!" I screamed.

"Both of you muthafuckas ruined my fucking life. I hate both of you. I hope both of y'all croak the fuck over."

"Oh, shut up with the dramatics you whore," Dara said before she started coughing uncontrollably. I was ready to go. This bitch was getting her nasty ass germs all up in my new Brazilian bundles.

"Come on now Karli and let me walk you out before you raise your mama's pressure." His dumb ass said.

I turned and walked out of the room and towards the

front door. In a way, I was glad that I came. I got a chance to see the person that I never wanted to turn into. When I stepped onto the porch, I heard Robert walk up behind me.

"Hey, you know that with your mama's situation, she won't be around much longer. Maybe we can rekindle that old flame that your mama made us put out." He said licking his crusty ass lips and looking me up and down; like if he had the chance, he would devour me right here on this porch.

"You got to be fucking kidding me. I would never let you touch me again nigga. You had the chance, and you chose my mama. You made the right choice though. You got me confused with the old Karli. This new Karli will beat the fuck out of you and steal your fucking SSI check. Do not call me again Robert. I don't care that Dara is sick. I don't care about anything that y'all have going on over here. It's not my problem." I said.

I got in my car and sped out of this fucking neighborhood. Fuck them, fuck Javier and anybody else that was against me.

I felt a sense of relief as I headed home to my man. I got rid of one of the problems that was intruding on my life. Now I just had to figure out what I was going to do about this other thing that was intruding on my life.

Antonio Henry

Emily and I were sitting in Eric's house on the couch after a night out. Even though I was tired and I wanted to be home with my wife, I needed to have this conversation with Eric more. I needed to be completely honest with him about how I felt and I needed my best friend Emily there for support

"Baby what's wrong? You look sad or deep in thought or something." Eric asked me while sitting next to me and rubbing my leg.

"I been thinking a lot lately Eric, and I think we can't do this anymore. I can't keep doing this to my wife. I love her, and I can't keep hurting her by doing what I'm doing with you. It's not fair to her. It's not fair to you either. You already know that even if my wife wasn't in the picture, that we still wouldn't be able to be together because of your father. It's just too many obstacles in our way, and I'm taking it as a sign that we need to slow down. I don't want to hurt you, but I have to finally do what I know is right," I said.

"So, these last few months have meant nothing to you? You're just going to throw me aside after you've used me up because you got your fix. You don't want me anymore?'' He cried.

"Eric, I hate to stick my nose in y'all business but

maybe you should just listen to him. You are very handsome and I know that you will find someone else that won't have so many strings attached to being with them, someone less complicated." Emily chimed in.

That's why I wanted her to be here. She was always the voice of reason

"These last few months have meant a lot to me. You give me things that Jazelle can't give me. But she also gives me things that you can't give me. You helped me realize who I really am. I'm a gay man deep down inside and I probably always will be. But, I'm also a man that is very much in love with a woman and my love for her trumps any and all things. I have feelings for you. But I am in love with her. She gave me a family and a life that I am proud of. I'm not willing to lose her behind me chasing something that I've been trying to leave behind for more than half of my life. I'm sorry Eric, but I have to let you go." I said raising up from my seat and starting towards the bathroom. I think I ate some bad oysters at dinner and I had to shit. "I'm going to go to the bathroom and then we are going to go ahead and leave."

It was getting too heated in there for me and I couldn't handle the look on his face when I let him down. I felt bad for having to do that but he wasn't worth the destruction that would come to my life if anybody other than Emily knew about what I had going on.

After handling my business in the bathroom, I threw some water on my face to try and shake myself up a little bit. I looked in the mirror and I looked dog ass tired. The bags under my eyes and the dark circles were proof that this life, all of my lies and my betrayal to my wife was taking a toll on me. I wasn't built for this shit and I wanted to go back to my normal life, back when my wife and I were happy and in love.

As I was walking back towards the living room, I could hear Emily and Eric having a hushed conversation.

"No! He can't leave me!!! I got rid of him for us. For Antonio and I!! We can be together now. All he has to do is leave Jazelle. We can adopt babies and be happy together. I can give him family too. I love him! I love him more than anything!! I don't know what I would do if he left me."

I was confused as hell. For one, he has never told me he loved me or that he needed me. It was always easy with him up until this point. I never felt pressured to be with him or anything. But he was giving me crazy vibes like a muthafucka. Then he said that he got rid of someone. What the fuck was his crazy ass talking about?

"Eric, what do you mean you got rid of him? What are you talking about?" Emily said taking the questions right out of my mind and verbalizing them.

"I killed my father so that Antonio and I could be together. I did it for us. So that we could live our lives together with no complications. Jazelle will get over it, and his girls will be fine because they will still see him. I can't live without Antonio. I can be his peace. I can be whatever he needs me to be."

I was about to walk in and interrupt his little confession but I thought better of it. Instead, I turned on my voice record app because I wanted to get this confession on the record just in case I had to use it against him. I was trying to let him down easy but he seemed like he was going to be a problem for me. This man was more emotional than any woman that I had ever met. So, I sat in the corner of the hall way and recorded their private conversation to cover my own ass in case shit went south

"Eric what the hell do you mean you killed your father? I thought that you said that he had a heart attack. You didn't say anything to me about him dying." Emily asked him.

"I poisoned him at breakfast a few weeks back. I put something in his drink that caused him to suffer from paralysis and then gave him a heart attack. The coroner ruled it a heart attack, and there was never an investigation. I had to do it. He would have never let me be who I really am. He would have never allowed Antonio and I to be together. But it was bigger than just him and me. I saved my mother and Sharise. I did a good thing. He deserved it," he explained to Emily

Wow! I was at a loss for words. I couldn't believe that he killed his father. Like Emily stated, he never told us that his father was dead. He just explained that he had a heart attack and that was all. I couldn't believe that he had gotten away with it. Now I really thought he was crazy and I knew that I needed to get away from him as soon as possible and cut all communication. I realized that he could ruin my life with a simple confession to my wife because why wouldn't he. I wasn't willing to give him what he wanted, and if he was capable of killing his own father, then he was capable of doing anything that he felt like he needed to do to in order to get what he wanted. That made him dangerous. And that meant that he had to go. I knew exactly what I had to do to rid myself of this crazy ass murderous man and get back to my life with my wife.

"Wow" Emily replied. Her voice ringing with exasperation. "That's some cold- hearted shit and now that you told me, you are bringing me into your shit. I love both you and Antonio but you never need to bring this shit up again, do you understand? I can't believe that you would do something like this for the love of a man that will never belong to you."

"I knew that you wouldn't understand. But I love him so much. We are going to be with each other forever. I can't wait." he said with an enthusiasm that he shouldn't have had in moment like this.

I had heard enough of this shit. Me and Emily were about to get the fuck up out of here.

"Emily are you ready to go?" I said walking back into the living room before they could continue their conversation. I wasn't going to let either one of them know that I knew what he had done.

To tell you the truth, a nigga was shook. I ain't never had to deal with no crazy ass man. Now I knew why God gave me Jazelle. Because this was not the life for me. Two men could never work. Not if the outcome was this. If he acted like this off of a few shots of good dick, I couldn't imagine if we were in a full-fledged relationship.

What the fuck did I get myself into.

Jazelle Henry

Donte had finally called me to meet up. I missed him so much, but while he was ignoring me, I was working on my relationship with my husband. Antonio had started spending more time at home, and I was starting to remember all of the reasons why I first fell in love with Antonio. He was attentive and kind and always put my wants and needs above his own.

But Donte still played a huge roll in my heart and my mind. For whatever reason, I still wanted him. I still needed him. I wanted him to feel the same about me, but he didn't. I could tell that something was up, and today I was going to find out who or what it was.

"What's up Jazelle?" he greeted me walking up to my table at the chick fil a we decided to meet at.

He usually greeted me with 'Hey baby' or 'Hey Pretty', but today, it was just Jazelle.

"Nothing's up with me Donte. But please tell me what the hell is up with you. You go missing for days at a time and pop back up on me like ain't nothing happened. On some real shit, I feel like you just straight up used me. You were giving me all of your time and attention when you wanted me to help you with something, but now that you don't need me anymore, I get nothing from you. I noticed this from the beginning, but I denied it because you gave me excitement and fun. You gave me all the things that Antonio didn't and I fell in love with you. Even though I knew it was wrong. Even though I knew that I was betraying my husband's trust. I still did it because you made me feel like I could. You made me feel like my heart would be safe with you. Now I know that I taught you exactly how to treat me. I gave you a fucking manual. I told you everything that I felt that I wasn't getting from Antonio and you did everything that he wasn't until it was no longer convenient for you. So please, you tell me what's up with you!!'' I said.

Over the last year, my heat had been through many ups and downs with the men that I loved. Antonio was finally starting to come around but I didn't know if he was still messing with Emily. If I hadn't complained about our marriage and actually tried to work on it, Emily wouldn't even exist. I was almost afraid to bring the situation up because if he lied to me about something that I had seen with my own eyes; it would piss me off. If he told me the truth, it would break my heart into a million more pieces. He still had no clue that I had been cheating on him, but I knew that very soon, I would have to tell him. We had both destroyed the sanctity of our marriage.

Donte had given me everything that I had ever thought that I wanted and now, he was slowly but surely taking it all away. How could he just come into my life and play with my heart. I wanted something that my husband wasn't giving me so bad, that I went out and found a replacement, only for the replacement to use me up and toss me out. But now it was too late. We would be bound together forever.

"Look Jazelle. I'm going, to be honest with you. I do like you. But I don't love you. I felt like you could bring things to my life that would help me, and you did. When I first met you, I already knew who you were. I work out with your husband he always talked about how perfect you were and how you helped him become a man. You did that for me too. I'm so thankful for everything that you have done for me. My life is so much better because of you. But I want you to try to work things out with your husband because I can't give you what you are asking of me. I can't give you my love because it already belongs to someone else.

My heart was broken. This nigga had some nerve telling me his loved belonged to someone else. After all that I had done, this is the thanks that I get. He handpicked me out of all of the bitches in the world that could have helped him. This selfish bitch made muthafucka used me and just expects me to move on. How fucking dare he treat me like I ain't worth shit.

I chuckled to myself. I had to laugh to keep from crying. I was pissed off more than I had ever been in my life. This entire relationship was a lie. Donte never cared about me. Hell, he couldn't have even liked me. If he did, using me would have never crossed his simple ass mind. But I couldn't be too mad since I was a married woman. I should have known that nothing good would come from my dirty deeds. I should have known that Karma would catch up with me. I couldn't expect him to want to settle down with a woman that was supposedly already settled. But that was my rational mind speaking. My broken heart spoke a different language. That's why I made sure that I would always be able to have him in my life one way or another. I had been hiding this secret from him for the last couple of months and it was about time that he found the fuck out.

"Well, good luck trying to be in love when you got a baby on the way. By the way, you start work on Monday at 11 am. You're definitely going to need that job now..... baby daddy." I smiled and got up to walk out of the restaurant.

I found out a month and a half ago that I was pregnant. And yes, it was definitely Donte's baby. Like I said Antonio and I weren't having sex until very recently. I was two months along, and I was keeping it. Donte could try to move on from me if he wanted to. But if he wanted to be a part of this baby's life, then he would be a part of mine also. After I watched my husband with Emily that night at Benihana's, Donte and I finally started having sex. I purposely stopped taking my birth control hoping that I would get pregnant. This way as long as Antonio forgave me for my infidelities, I could always have my cake and eat it too. My plan worked, and I was happy. So, whoever he was giving his love to, I hoped that she was prepared to share him.

He didn't need to tell me to work things out with my husband because I was already doing that. But I would have Donte too, rather he wanted me or not.

After leaving Chick Fil A, I was on my way to my doctor's appointment to check on me and Donte's baby. I pulled up to Baylor Scott and White Andrews Women's Hospital in Ft. Worth after about a twenty-minute drive. I walked in to the building and checked myself in at the front desk. The lady gave me a clipboard with a thick ass packet and asked me to fill out all of the information since this was my first time at this office.

I didn't know how I was going to break this news to Antonio that I was pregnant with another man's baby. I felt horrible, but we were both cheating on each other, so hopefully, he would forgive me like I planned to forgive him for cheating on me with Emily.

After filling out the paperwork, I took the clipboard back to the front desk then returned to my seat and waited to be called back. It was just my luck that little husband stealing bitch Emily walks into the office and goes to the front desk.

She better not be pregnant by my damn husband or they were going to see another side of me. I thought to myself This woman was beautiful as she strutted across the doctor's office. I almost felt too insecure to approach her. No one had ever made me feel less than before. But with my new found discovery that Donte was using me from the beginning and the fact that my husband was cheating on me also, I wasn't confident in myself at all. Still, this was a situation that I needed to deal with and quickly. I got up from my seat to go and sit next to her. This bitch had the nerve to hold on to her purse as if I was a smooth fucking criminal and was going to snatch her purse out of her lap.

"Hi. I'm Jazelle. Antonio's wife. Your name is Emily, right?" I asked her.

"Yes, it is. How may I help you?" she replied.

How may I help you??? You got to be shitting me. This woman was turning up her nose at me and talking to me like I was beneath her.

"Well, since you don't seem to be in the mood for small talk, I'll get straight to the point. I just so happened to be at a restaurant a few weeks back, and I saw you all cozied up to my husband. I want to know what the hell you have going on with my man, and I want it to stop. I don't know about you, but I'm not into sharing what's mine," I said angrily.

This bitch had the unmitigated gall to laugh at me. She laughed hard like I was Kevin Hart and she was front and center at my damn show.

"Honey trust me when I say that I am not the one that you need to be worried about. I am not Barbara, and you are not Shirley, so please don't come to me as a woman. If you have an issue with your man stepping out on you, then you need to have a conversation with your man and not me. I can't do nothing for you, sweetie."

"JAZELLE HENRY," the nurse called out to me.

"Look, bitch. I am the wrong wife to piss off. If you know what's good for you, you will back the fuck away from my husband." I said before I got up and followed the nurse into one of the exam rooms. I was pissed off, but I knew that I needed to keep my stress low for my baby.

After getting some sonogram pictures and the doctor telling me that my little bundle of joy was doing great, I headed back to the waiting room to get my next appointment. Emily was already gone.

I walked back to my car and noticed that there was a piece of paper tucked under my windshield wipers. I picked it up to throw it because I assumed it was one of those club flyers that some promotor put on my car trying to get people to turn up in a hole in the wall club with musty bathrooms and watered-down liquor. But when I picked it up, I saw my name scribbled across the front. I unfolded the piece of paper to read it.

Stay away from my man bitch.

He is mine.

Pack your bags and leave or else.

This was the second note that I had gotten from this crazy bitch. She really wanted my husband that bad that she would threaten me. I stuffed the note into my purse and went to get into the car. I started my car and tried to back out of my parking spot, but my car was stalling or something. I got out of the car to check and see what was wrong with my car. I walked around the back and seen that my back-driver side tire was slashed. I checked all of the other tires, and they were all flat except for the front driver side tire. This bitch was a professional tire slasher. I definitely had to confront Antonio about this. Because I didn't feel like being harassed by my husband's mistress.

Antonio and I were going out to eat tonight because he wanted me to meet a friend of his. That reminded me that I needed to call Karli to invite her. Hopefully, it wouldn't be like the last double date that we went on. But after dinner tonight, I would be confronting tony about his little side bitch because she was out of control.

177

Eric Sawyer

I've been so busy consoling my mother, that I hardly had time for anything else these days. She was still distraught over my father's death. I couldn't understand why she was so hurt when she was a victim just like me. He hurt her just like he hurt me, and I thought that by killing him, I was helping her get her life back. But she was making me feel like shit for doing what I felt like was the right thing.

"I just can't believe that he's gone. He was healthy, and I just can't believe that his heart all of a sudden gave up on him. I don't know what to do without him, Eric. I don't know how to live," she cried.

She was bugging the shit out of me. I had other things to deal with like the fact that Antonio was trying to go ghost on me. He was trying to leave me after all of the sacrifices I made to be with him. I was trying to figure out a way to get him to stay with me; I couldn't come up with anything. He was adamant about staying with his wife and doing right by her.

Donte had explained to me that he was meeting Jazelle to try and break things off with her. That definitely wasn't going to work in my favor with getting her away from my man. I had been doing little things like slashing her tires and leaving notes on her car. I was trying to scare her away from him and judging from her reaction at the clinic from seeing her tires slashed, I could tell that it was affecting her. Which is exactly what I wanted.

"I know mom, but he's in a better place now. He's with God. I know that you have to grieve, but I also want you to think about how much freedom you will have now. You'll be able to think like you want and act like you want. You will be able to be the woman you used to be before you married him," I said to her.

"That's just it son, I don't want to be that woman. Yes, your father could be mean and abusive sometimes, but he gave me everything. Before him, I was a drugged-out street walker until he picked me up and cleansed me from my wicked whorish ways. I loved him for that. No matter how many times he hit me or cursed at me, he still saved me. I owe him everything," she told me.

Damn, I didn't know all of that. But it was already done, he was gone and he wasn't coming back.

"I'm sorry mom."

"I know baby, I'm going to your spare room to take a nap. I'm tired and have a headache from all of this crying. I'll see you later son." She said as she got up and headed to the bedroom.

Damn my life was fucked up. Even Sharise was pissed at me when I called her and told her that we were done for good and that she should go and live her life without me. But I knew that it was better for her that way.

KNOCK KNOCK KNOCK

I went to see who was at my door. I looked through the peephole and saw Donte standing on the other side of my door. He didn't tell me he was coming, but I could use the company.

"Aye, what's up man. What brings you this way?" I said opening the door wider to allow him entry into my home.

"I just got that text from Antonio on where we are having dinner tonight. I figured that we could just ride there together." He said taking a seat on the couch.

"Oh yea, this came at just the right time cause my mother is blowing me with all this crying about my father's death."

"Nigga that was her husband, of course, she is gone be fucked up about him dying suddenly, and you should be a little more sympathetic also. You acting like you don't give a fuck that your dad is gone," he said.

"Oh, I guess you feeling all high and mighty since you finally broke up with the married woman that you were using. Get the fuck outta here nigga. You should be showing her some sympathy," I said.

"Fuck all that, you gone get dressed or what so we

can roll? I'm trying to be there a little early." Donte said changing the subject because he knew I was right.

"Alright let me go shower and get dressed. Thirty minutes tops," I said jogging to my room.

Antonio didn't invite me to dinner with him, but he invited Donte. That was fucked up to me. We were way closer than them two, but he was determined to leave me out. I couldn't wait to see the look on his face when I popped up on his ass.

Thirty minutes later I was ready to go. Donte and I jumped in his whip and headed to Ruth Chris Steak House in Dallas.

Antonio Henry

"Hurry up Jazelle! We are going to dinner, not a fashion show." I yelled to my wife who was upstairs still getting dressed after 3 hours. I couldn't stand how long it took her to get dressed, but I always loved the way she looked when she finally came down the stairs.

"I'm almost done Tony damn! Just wait. That damn steak house gone still be there whenever we get there," she said

She had been kind of snippy since she got back home earlier. I mean she had been snapping on me for the smallest things. Maybe it was that time of the month for her, and her hormones were all out of whack or something.

"I'll be in the car. I gave my friend a specific time, and I don't want to be too late," I said.

I grabbed my keys from the bowl on the table and headed to the car and started it up. We usually take Jazelle's car when we go out somewhere, but she said that she had to get the car towed for a flat tire earlier. I don't know why she just didn't call me to change it for her. Jazelle and I had been doing so much better, and I wanted her to know that she could still count on me.

While I was sitting in the car waiting on Jazelle, Emily text my phone. When I looked at what she sent me, I got nervous as hell. My hands got sweaty, and my throat became dry.

Emily: Your wife confronted me today and told me to stay away from you. She thinks we're fucking.

Antonio: What?! Where did you see my wife? What exactly does she know? What did you tell her?

I was just texting question after question. How could my wife possibly know about Emily? The only thing that I could think of was that Karli's ghetto trash ass told her. Ugh! I hated that funky ass bitch.

Emily: She said that she seen us at dinner together with her own eyes. She said that we were cozied up on each other which probably meant that we were alone.

I could only think of one time that Emily and I had dinner alone in the past five months.

Antonio: The only time that we were alone was when we went to Benihanas and Eric had cancelled on us.

Emily: Exactly!!!!

FUCKKKK! I know this crazy ass dude wasn't trying to throw me under the bus. I guess I shouldn't put it past him though. The nigga did kill his own father just so he could be gay out in the open.

Antonio: Do you think that he would do that though?

Emily: I was with you when you tried to break up with him. It's possible. Look there's something else. When I was leaving the clinic where your wife confronted me, I seen that she had all her tires slashed. So be careful friend.

Antonio: I will. Thanks for the info.

What the fuck was Jazelle doing at a clinic? Did Eric have something to do with her tires and shit being slashed? What the hell was really going on? All these secrets were starting to take a toll on me. I couldn't even remember the lie I told this morning, let alone all the lies that I've told over the past year. This was becoming too much.

Jazelle finally made her way to the car. She got in and buckled herself in without saying a word to me. Now I understood the reason why she had been snapping at me all day. I knew that I was in deep shit. I had to get out.

Donte Abraham

Eric and I arrived at the restaurant about 20 minutes before we were supposed to be there. We were seated and waiting on our unsuspecting guests.

Watching the look on Jazelle's face when she finally walked into the restaurant was fucking hilarious. I already told her that I knew Antonio, so I don't know why she was too surprised.

"Uhhhh, Donte. I didn't know you were bringing Eric along with you," Antonio said when he approached the table.

"What's up man?" he nodded towards Eric.

"Yea it was last minute," Eric responded.

"This is my wife, Jazelle. Jazelle, this is Eric and Donte. I work out with them from time to time," Antonio said.

"Hello to you both," Jazelle spoke to the both of us in her usual soft melodic voice.

She couldn't even look me in the face. She was nervous as hell. I guess she never expected us all to be in the same room. I knew all along that it would happen at some point.

I still couldn't believe that her ass was pregnant. Hopefully, she was just lying to piss me off and get under my skin for breaking things off with her. But if she was indeed pregnant, then I knew that the baby was mine. I was going to take care of my baby and be in his or her life rather Antonio liked it or not. That's if they even stayed together after he found out that she was pregnant by me. I was scared as fuck to tell Karli because I told her that I wasn't even having sex with Jazelle anymore. I didn't want Mya to find out cause that bitch might just cut my dick off.

Finally, our last guest arrived. My baby Karli sauntered her fine ass in here like she owned this bitch.

She walked over to where I was sitting and kissed me dead ass in the mouth. In front of her best friend. I didn't give a fuck about Jazelle knowing, but I didn't think that Karli wanted to hurt her friend like I'm sure she had just done.

I looked up at Jazelle, and her eyes welled up with tears. Looking at her, I did feel a little bad. Like I said I liked her energy and everything, she just wasn't my type. That didn't mean I wanted to cause her pain. I just fell in love with her friend. I couldn't control that.

"I'm going to the restroom," Jazelle said as she abruptly stood up and walked away.

"I'ma go with her," Karli said as she kissed me again then got up and walked after Jazelle. This shit was gone be bad.

"Hi. My name is Amber and I'll be your server

tonight. Can I take your drink orders?" A cute little blonde waitress approached us.

"I'll have a Hennessey and Lemonade and the same for my girlfriend," I ordered.

"I'll have a water and an Apple martini for my wife please," Antonio ordered.

"Oh. No Crown and coke for you tonight huh," Eric directed his question to Antonio.

"Well Ms. Amber, I'll order a crown and coke for myself then thank you," Eric said very flamboyantly might I add.

That shit had me looking at the both of them funny

Karli Washington

"Look Jazelle. I'm sorry," I said to her after we entered the ladies' room.

"Sorry for what Karli. Sorry for stealing my man or sorry for being a sorry ass friend."

"I'm sorry that you feel like I'm a sorry ass friend. But he was never your man. Hell, to be honest, he ain't even my man. That's a married man and until he gets divorced, he's only her man. You can't be mad at me Jazelle. I'm sorry for betraying you, but I love him, and I'm not going to stop loving him. You are married to Antonio. That's where you need to be." I said.

"I know who the fuck I'm married to Karli and what the fuck are you talking about? Donte is not married. I know everything about him and I know for a fact that he's a single man.

I wanted to laugh at her stupid ass. This bitch was so smart that she was dumb. She was so fucking confident in Donte that she never thought to look past the obvious bullshit.

"Jazelle, I've been to this man's home. Have you? Has he ever invited you to the place that he lays his head every night? You know damn well that he hasn't, because if he did then you would know that he has a fucking wife." I said to her stupid ass.

She couldn't possibly be this clueless. How could she be dealing with a man for damn near a year and have absolutely no idea that he was married. She ignored all of the red flags when it came to Donte. It's like he had her brain warped or something. All she saw was what she wanted to see. She didn't see the things that she needed to see.

"Well, I hope that both of you bitches are willing to share him. Because I'm two months pregnant by Donte and I'm not getting rid of my baby," she said shocking the hell out of me for a second.

But the more I thought about it, the more I didn't believe her.

I didn't believe her. This bitch took her birth control faithfully and had been since her last baby was born. She said that she did not want any more kids. Donte had even told me that he wasn't even having sex with her lying ass. So, I knew her ass was bluffing, but I would definitely play along.

"Well, congratulations bitch. I guess we finally get what we always said we wanted in high school. We get to be pregnant together," I said and walked out of the restroom and back towards the table. Fuck this shit. I didn't have time for Jazelle and her little mind games.

I was really pregnant, and I was considering an abortion because I felt like I was still a little too selfish to be a mother. But since my petty meter went higher than my selfish meter. I was going to keep this baby just to prove to Jazelle that Donte was going to be mine, and there was nothing that she could do about it. I walked back over to Donte to tell I'm that I was making an early exit. I was already over this night, plus I had a workout scheduled for early in the morning with Emily, and I wanted to be well rested.

"Hey baby, I'm going to go ahead and head out. I have an early morning and want to sleep." I said to him. I was only six weeks pregnant and this baby was already snatching my damn energy.

"Alright, I will see you in the morning." He said and then he kissed me like he didn't really want me to leave. Leaving was the best move to make right now because I know that if I didn't leave, I was going to have to slap the shit out of Jazelle.

I got up and headed to my car. She should have told me that Donte was going to be there. Or he should have told me that he was going to have dinner with Antonio and Jazelle. He said absolutely nothing to me about meeting them. Somebody should have kept a bitch in the loop. But me and Donte's secret was going to come out sooner or later. I hated to be the woman that betrayed her best friend of 14 years. But I couldn't help who I loved.

Eric Sawyer

Antonio was pissed the fuck off that I showed up to his little dinner that he purposely didn't invite me to. But I gave no fucks. He was going to fall into line and give me the attention that I wanted, or I was going to let his wife know that he wasn't cheating with Emily but fucking the shit out of me.

The only reason that I didn't confront him was because Donte was at the table also and I wasn't ready to come out to him.

I could feel my sanity slipping more and more. The more that Antonio ignored and denied me, the crazier my thoughts got. I wanted him more than anything and that was all that I could see. I had tunnel vision. It was like a sick obsession that I had with Antonio, because I felt like he was the only person who had ever fully accepted me for who I was. For him to give me that and then try to snatch it away because he was afraid of what society would think if they knew who he really was, was unacceptable to me.

Jazelle had finally found her way back to the table, and she looked as if she had been crying. I'm assuming this is her first time learning that Donte and Karli were now together. I guess that she never even found out that the nigga was married too. Poor girl couldn't catch a break. Neither one of her men could be faithful to her. But it was her fault. She invited all of Donte's drama into her life, so she had to put on her big girl panties and deal with the fact that she betrayed her husband for a man that wasn't even good enough for her.

I decided to make Antonio sweat a little more, so I pulled out my phone and sent him a text.

Eric: If you won't love me, I'm going to tell your wife about us. ☐

I watched him look at his phone, and a look of disappointment or anger or some emotion that I had never seen on him crossed his face.

Antonio: Meet me at our usual hotel room tomorrow night at 7 pm. I'm going to give you what you been missing because you are acting up.

I was happy as fuck. I just knew that he was gone fuck me right back into my happy place.

Eric: Okay baby. See you then.

I just stuffed my phone back into my pocket and acted accordingly for the remainder of the night. Dinner went smoothly, and Jazelle never suspected a thing. Donte seemed to be looking at the both of us a little funny, but I couldn't be worried about that right now. I was happy that I was going to be able to see my man tomorrow.

Emily Medrano

I couldn't believe that Antonio's wife had confronted me yesterday. She definitely had shit all wrong though. Antonio and I were just really good friends and because of that, I failed to uphold my womanly duties of protecting another woman from what I knew was a danger that was lurking and just waiting to make its move. I wanted to tell her who she should be worried about but I didn't want to blow up Antonio's secret. He would tell her when he was ready. I knew that it was Eric's crazy ass that had slashed her tires and I knew that if he did not get what he wanted, that things would get worse. I couldn't be mad at her for confronting me. She thought that I was sleeping with her husband and I personally knew how she felt. I knew what it felt like to have the man you love cheat on you.

I've have been knowing that Javier had been cheating on me for a while now. I never said anything or confronted him about it because I wanted to handle things my own way. I hired a private investigator, and she brought me back the proof that I needed. I was never the type of woman to react off of hearsay or a suspicion that I might have had. I always needed cold hard facts. So, when I found out that it was Karli's trashy ass that was sneaking around with my man I was pissed. I had allowed this woman into my home. We had built a rapport, and I thought that we had become friends. All along this bitch had my husband wrapped around her finger. His call logs confirmed that he would call her all times of the day and night. He was meeting up with the bitch at hotel rooms and lying to me so that he could go. I couldn't believe that he would cheat on me with someone like her. She was loud and trashy and the complete opposite of me.

Mya was my client and also a really close friend of mine. She confided in me that one of my clients had also been sleeping with her husband. She said that she had seen her before leaving a session with me. Mya had been suspecting her man of cheating also, so she had cameras set up throughout her house to try and catch him. When she brought me the videos, I was surprised to see that not only had Karli been sleeping with my husband, but she was also sleeping with Donte, Mya's husband. Donte was dumb enough to actually bring that bitch to Mya's house and fuck her like she was his wife.

I thought about just telling her that I couldn't be her trainer anymore and being done with her, but that wouldn't stop her from sleeping with Javier. So, I decided to keep her on as a client to keep her close so that I could have my revenge on the bitch.

"What time is she supposed to be here?'' Mya asked.

"She should be here in the next ten minutes. Look, just act normal. Don't jump on the bitch as soon as she arrives. We have to play this smart. She doesn't know that either of us know about her being a stank hoe and sleeping with our husbands. We just gone beat her ass a little bit, and then let her be on her way. Hopefully, she will learn to keep her pussy to herself," I said.

"Girl I'm going to try, but this bitch got some nerve fucking all over my house like her name is on the damn deed."

"Tell me about it. But she will get what's coming to her," I said. Just as I finished my sentence, I heard my doorbell ring.

DING DONG

"I'll get it," I said to Mya as I headed to the front of my house to answer the door.

Lights Camera Action Bitch

Karli Washington

After I left that little fucked up dinner party last night, I went home feeling really messed up about my actions. I thought that I was becoming a better woman, but my actions were proving me wrong. Donte made me want to be better, but I was still hurting my friend. I was still treating her like I treated everyone else in my life, like she didn't matter to me. I hated that my happiness caused her pain. I didn't want to be the cause of her unhappiness, but I also didn't want her infatuation with Donte to cause mine. I had never been as happy as I am right now. I couldn't continue to hide my love for him which is why I kissed him in front of her like that and told her that he was married. I was hoping that the news would cause her to want to leave him alone. It seemed easier than trying to speak to her about my feelings for him knowing that she would have no understanding. Javier was no longer stalking me, and I was finally getting the love that I longed for when I was with Robert.

If Jazelle was indeed pregnant with Donte's baby, which I didn't believe, I don't know how that was going to play out for any of us. It would definitely be bad for everybody. Especially me. That meant that she would always be in his life and that I could never have him to myself.

I had woken up early to get ready for my appointment

with Emily. She insisted that I come in today instead of my regular day because she wouldn't be available for the rest of the week. As I was putting on my workout clothes, I received a text from Donte.

Donte: Good Morning Beautiful. What are your plans for today?

Karli: I have a session with Emily, and then I'm yours for the rest of the day.

Donte: That's what I like to hear. I got a surprise for you.

Karli: A surprise? What is it?

Donte: I will let you know when I see you later.

Karli: Ugh ok. I got something that I need to talk to you about anyways. I'm going to share my location with you so that you will know where I will be. TTYL

After I finished getting dressed, I headed over to Emily's

DING DONG

I waited at the door a minute or so before Emily answered.

"Hey, girl. We are in the back. Come on in," she said letting me into the house.

"We?" I asked.

"We have someone else joining us?" I asked annoyed.

I saw the other car in the driveway but I just assumed that the bitch had a new car or something. She could afford to with all the money I was paying her per session.

I liked to work out without the company of bitches I didn't know, and Emily knew that.

"Yes, my other client Mya. I had to have her come in today also because as I informed you yesterday, I won't be available for the rest of the week," she responded with a little attitude in her voice.

"Whatever. Let's get this over with!" I said walking to the back of the house where her little workout gym room was

I didn't know what her attitude was about but she needed to fix that shit expeditiously.

"Let's," she said from behind me.

When I walked into the room, there was another woman there. She looked so familiar to me. I had seen her before somewhere. Suddenly it came to me, I seen her on a picture on her mantle in her home. This was Donte's wife.

She turned around and smiled at me, and I realized that I had seen her here before also. She was the woman walking into Emily's house the day that I met Javier. This was definitely a small world after all.

"Ok ladies let us begin our workout," Emily said standing in front of both of us.

"Before we begin our workout, I got a question." Donte's wife spoke up.

"Where have I seen you before?'' She asked turning towards me.

"I don't know. Probably here leaving one of my workouts," I replied.

"No. No. I don't think that's it," she said. "It was somewhere else."

"Well if you so fucking sure, what the fuck you asking me for? You obviously already know that you saw me somewhere. Gone on with them games and shit. A bitch done changed but I aint changed that damn much." I said ready to slap this bitch. It was obvious that she knew she saw me before. The bitch was acting like she had a fucking problem with me or something. Both of these bitches were on one today.

Suddenly, a thought came to me.

Wait did this bitch know about me fucking her husband?

"Yes, bitch! We both know that you are fucking both of our husbands,'' Emily said.

Shit. I thought I had said that only to myself. I always had a problem with thinking out loud. But that was the least of my problems. I hadn't been confronted about sleeping with someone's man since my mama caught me, and Robert together. I didn't know what was about to happen, but I did know that if these bitches wanted smoke then I was gone give these bitches smoke and that was on my dying mama.

"Well, I'm not the person that y'all need to be mad at. I ain't got no loyalty to either one of you hoes. Check ya nigga. I'm out this bitch." I said trying to walk out of the room.

Before I could get to the door, Mya ran to the door and shut the fucking door and locked it. She turned around and faced me with a sinister ass smile on her face.

These bitches were about to jump me. These hoes really wanted to fight me over these niggas that obviously didn't want them. I backed up to where my back was against the wall, and prepared myself to windmill the shit out of these crazy bitches.

They stood on either side of me like two lionesses stalking their prey. I ain't even gone lie, I was kind of scared. I could fight any bitch one on one, but these bitches were a package deal. They were giving out two for one specials.

Next thing I know Mya ass screamed to the top of her lungs and jumped on me like a damn banshee spider monkey or some shit. She started to pummel me in my head until I fell to the ground. I didn't even have time to even think about fighting back. She had caught me completely off guard with that loud ass scream. She continued to punch me in my face over and over again. This bitch was strong as fuck, her punches felt like Kimbo Slice was knocking my shit back and not this small ass woman that was no taller than 5'3 and weighed no more than 130 pounds.

When I hit the ground, Emily came and started to kick me in my face. She had on them big ass FILAS that looked like orthopedic shoes. She was kicking me so hard that I was leaking from my nose and my mouth. This bitch has kicked gashes into my face with these big ass dinosaur shoes. I could feel myself trying to pass out. But I knew that I needed to stay strong so that once they were done, I could crawl my ass back to the safety of my vehicle and hopefully call someone to help me.

But they were relentless.

They were not stopping.

All that I could do was protect my belly because for the first time, I was concerned about someone other than myself. I couldn't be worried about my own safety right now because I had something precious growing inside of me. Something that was made out of love. I managed to turn myself over onto my stomach so that they could no longer kick me there.

And then it stopped.

I thought I was in the clear.

I thought they were done

"Mya no! That's too far. We already beat the shit out her. Let's just let her go." I could hear Emily panicking in the background.

"Naw fuck that shit. This bitch ain't gone learn. She gone continue to do the same shit! She can not have my fucking husband!" Mya responded.

"Put that dumbbell down Mya. Let the bitch go," Emily said again.

The first hit, I felt everything. I felt the pain from my head where she struck me, all the way to my toes. I screamed to the top of my lungs in hopes that someone would come and save me. But that was wishful thinking. The second and third hits, I didn't feel at all. I was already numb. I knew that I wasn't going to make it through this. And in my 30 years of life, I couldn't think of one thing that I didn't regret, except for my baby, that I was sure that I was never going to meet. I would never get the chance to apologize to Jazelle. She was my only friend and I never should have done her how I did. I had spent way too much time being jealous of her when I just should have been happy for her like I know that she would have been for me had I not been a sneaky bitch. I wanted to apologize to my mother and even Emily. All of the decisions that I have ever made led me to this point. It was over for me. Look at what love had done to me.

HE WASN'T GOOD ENOUGH FOR ME

Antonio Henry

After dinner last night, Jazelle and I went home but didn't even bother to speak to each other. I knew that she was pissed at me because of the Emily situation but I was too scared to even bring it up. I knew that she wanted to speak to me about it but right now I had to go out and handle some things. I wanted to ask her what she was doing at the clinic, but I didn't have the right to question her on anything. After all I was the one that was cheating. But tonight, after I was done with Eric, we both had to sit down and have a serious conversation.

Tonight, Eric was going to meet me at the W in downtown Dallas which was the hotel that we usually met up at when we couldn't go to his home. Since his mother had been staying with him, his home was unavailable to us which kind of made what I had to do a tad bit harder. I still had his confession from killing his father saved to my phone, and it just so happens that my brother is a Detective with the Dallas Police Department. I had been saving it for this very moment because I was no fool, and I knew this day would come. I knew that he would push me this far.

Some may think that turning that information over to

my brother was extreme. But desperate times caused for desperate measures. If I didn't get rid of Eric, he was for sure going to blow my cover and send my whole entire world crashing down before my eyes. He was already sending me threatening text messages talking about if I didn't fuck him that he was going to tell Jazelle about everything that we had going on and according to Emily he was slashing my wife's tires and shit. I knew that he has set Emily and I up and told Jazelle where we were going to be, trying to make it seem like I was cheating with Emily.

I was just starting to get back on my wife's good side and he had to go and fuck that up for me. I couldn't give him another opportunity to fuck up my home. I couldn't let him wreck my life any more than he already had. This is what I get though. I knew that Eric would be bad for me but at that point I couldn't let him go. Now, that one decision was coming back to bite me in the ass. Truth was, Eric was never enough for me. He encompassed what I needed in the physical form, but that was it. Jazelle encompassed everything. She was everything that I needed. And I wish I would have known the things that I know now. I would have never decided to move forward with Eric. It was one thing to think it, but it was another thing to act on it. And that was where I fucked up. I was learning that the grass was definitely not greener on the other side. And since I made this mess, it was about time that I cleaned it up.

I walked through the house looking for Jazelle. I wanted to tell her that I loved her and that I would be stepping out for a little while. I caught her in the bathroom throwing up what seemed like everything that she had eaten.

"What's wrong with you? Are you sick?" I asked her.

"I'm fine Tony. I probably just got food poisoning from the restaurant last night." She replied while spitting into the toilet.

"Do you need some help?"

"No, I'm fine. What do you want?" She asked looking up at me.

"I just wanted to let you know that I was going to step out for a little bit, but I should be back soon," I said.

"Mhmmm ok. I'll see you later then," she replied while rolling her eyes.

"I won't go if you don't want me to. You already know that I don't mind staying home and taking care of you," I told her.

Even though I meant it, I was hoping that she didn't want me to stay.

"It's ok Tony. I will be fine. The girls are already

down for their nap, so I will just take a nap too until they wake up." She said raising up from the toilet and walking over to the sink to rinse her mouth out.

"Alright, I'll see you later," I said kissing her forehead and walking out of the bathroom.

I grabbed the keys to my cars and left my house. My first stop would be to my brother's office to discuss our plan. I called him to let him know that I was on my way.

Once I made it to his office, we discussed how it would go down. Since I had already booked the hotel room. I had already gone and picked up the key. I gave one to my brother so that he could just walk up in that bitch on his police shit and get Eric the fuck up out of there.

I sat at my brother's office until it was time for me to make my way over to the room. I wanted to be there before Eric so that I could get the room and myself together. I already knew that he was going to want to have sex and I was going to indulge in him one last time. It was stupid, I know that. But it was just one more time and he would be out of my life for good.

I sat around the room nervous as hell for about twenty minutes before he arrived.

KNOCK KNOCK KNOCK

I went and opened the door for him. He walked past me into the room and sat on the bed facing me.

"I'm glad that you showed up like you said you would," he smiled at me.

"Yea, me too." Taking a seat in the chair that was next to the bed.

"I'm sorry that I have been acting kind of crazy lately. I've just been missing you like crazy. I never want to go so long without feeling you ever again. I know you missed me too. That's why you really showed up." He said while taking off his jacket and shirt.

"Yea you right. I should've never told you that I wanted to end what we have going on. It's just that I can't leave Jazelle right now. Our girls are still young, and they need the both of us." I lied to him.

This muthafucka was crazy. But I was going to play his little game until my brother, and his officers showed up. I didn't want this nigga to flip out and kill me next.

"I already told you that your girls will be ok and that Jazelle will get over it. Come take a seat on the bed."

Hesitantly I got up to move over to the bed. As soon as I took a seat, he immediately began to unbuckle my pants. He was rushing so much, I felt like I was being violated. He was completely taking control of the situation.

Once he got my pants down to my ankles, he kneeled down in front of me and took my whole dick into his mouth. My body visibly relaxed as Eric gave me some of the best head I had ever had. It's always the crazy ones with the good head game. I leaned back on my elbows and let my head fall back as I enjoyed him this one last time. I grabbed the back of his head and thrust my dick further into his mouth. I was so into it that I didn't even hear the door to the hotel room open.

"OH MY GOD ANTONIO!!! WHAT THE FUCK ARE YOU DOING?? What the fuck is this??? You're GAY??! Are you Fucking GAY??? Is that Eric!!! What the fuck do you motherfuckers having going on?" Jazelle yelled from the entrance of the door.

I jumped up and stumbled all over myself trying to pull my pants back up and gain my composure. How the fuck did she know that I was going to be here?

"It's not what it looks like baby! I promise! It's not what it looks like." I pleaded.

I didn't know what the fuck else to say because it was exactly what it looked like. I was sitting in a hotel room, enjoying oral sex from a man, and my wife had caught me. FUCK!!! What was I supposed to do now?

I looked over to Eric, and his bitch ass was sitting over there with a fucking smirk on his face. Jazelle turned and ran out of the room. I wanted to follow her, but before I could find my bearings, I heard.

"Eric Sawyer, you have the right to remain Silent. Anything you say can and will be used against you in the court of law. You have the right to an attorney. If you cannot afford an attorney, one will be provided for you." One of the officers said while hemming Eric up against the wall to handcuff him.

"What the fuck is this about? Why are you arresting me? You have to tell me why you are arresting me!" Eric screamed.

"You are under arrest for the murder of Pastor Earnest Sawyer." The officer stated.

Eric just looked over to me with tears in his eyes and all I could do was smile. That part was over. But little did I know; my problems were just beginning.

To Be Continued

CPSIA information can be obtained
at www.ICGtesting.com
Printed in the USA
LVHW031542310719
626019LV00002B/252